A Candlelight Ecstasy Romance®

"I'VE GOT TO HAND IT TO YOU. YOU HAD ME FOOLED," PIERRE SAID ANGRILY.

"What do you mean?" Jen stiffened. She'd never seen Pierre Rennes, one of the preeminent chefs of France, so angry.

"I wouldn't have thought you capable of it, but I'd say you've been using me in this little romantic adventure. I know how competitive these cooking classes are. You think I don't know how much it means to come in first? All the publicity, the gold seal alone could be instrumental in helping an aspiring restauranteur set up a successful business!"

"How could you think I'd do that? I love you!" Jen was on the verge of tears.

"Don't play the victim with me. If you tell me the truth, then maybe we can salvage what's left of our relationship. Just admit you got involved with me for your own selfish purposes. You've used me, Jenifer, why can't you admit it?"

CANDLELIGHT ECSTASY ROMANCES®

A TASTE OF HEAVEN

Samantha Hughes

A CANDLELIGHT ECSTASY ROMANCE®

Published by
Dell Publishing Co., Inc.
1 Dag Hammarskjold Plaza
New York, New York 10017

ISBN: 0-440-18506-8

Printed in the United States of America

First Printing—July 1985

To Our Readers:

We have been delighted with your enthusiastic response to Candlelight Ecstasy Romances®, and we thank you for the interest you have shown in this exciting series.

In the upcoming months we will continue to present the distinctive, sensuous love stories you have come to expect only from Ecstasy. We look forward to bringing you many more books from your favorite authors and also, the very finest work from new authors of contemporary romantic fiction.

As always, we are striving to present the unique, absorbing love stories that you enjoy most—books that are more than ordinary romance. Your suggestions and comments are always welcome. Please write to us at the address below.

Sincerely,

The Editors
Candlelight Romances
1 Dag Hammarskjold Plaza
New York, New York 10017

CHAPTER ONE

Jenifer Mallory walked briskly along the banks of the Seine, her cheeks flushed and stinging from the cool damp air. Imagine people back in Duffy warning her about jet lag! Jet lag in Paris?

"Go straight to your hotel," Meryl Beamen, the elderly librarian, had advised her, "and sleep for two hours. Don't sleep any longer! Then get up, walk around a bit and go back to bed." Meryl was her mother's cousin twice removed and the un-questioned authority on world travel in Duffy, Iowa.

Jen grinned as she thought of all the advice she'd been given since winning the Bradley National Bake-off and being awarded a trip to France to study cooking with three-star chef Pierre Rennes. It was funny, really, because most of Duffy's two thousand citizens hadn't been farther east than Chicago.

There was no way Jen could have gone directly to her hotel and pulled the covers over her head for a two-hour nap! From the moment the plane touched down at de Gaulle airport at dawn she had felt a wild fluttering in her stomach.

After checking into her modest hotel across from the Jardin des Tuileries she set out through the deserted gardens. They were still verdant and lush despite the autumnal nip in the air. As the city came alive and the morning traffic honked and snarled, Jen made her way past the fashionable shops along the Champs Élysées, circling up to the Madeleine and back down to the Place de la Concorde, where she walked along the river. From time to time she dug her hands into the pockets of her raincoat to consult her guidebook or her dog-eared French dictionary, a relic from her Duffy High School days.

Paris was bathed in autumn mists, not exactly an ideal day for walking, but it suited Jen perfectly. The sight of Notre-Dame's Gothic spires brought tears to her eyes. She was unabashedly sentimental and each famous landmark stirred within her a deep sense of optimism.

Her life was changing. *She* was making it change. If anyone had told her five years ago—no, even two years ago—that she would be walking *alone* along the Quai du Louvre, she would have laughed. The idea of being alone in a foreign city was something beyond the realm of possibility for the woman she had been two years ago.

And now it seemed the most natural thing in the world. Of course she would miss the children. She was prepared for moments of weakness, for encroaching guilt. But the decision had been hers alone and in her heart she knew it was the right decision. The boys were safe and secure on her parents' farm just outside Duffy. Mike, the oldest at nine, was sleeping in her old girlhood room.

10

They were all much better off on the farm than they had been in the dismal cramped tract home outside Des Moines in the tense months before Ed had asked for a divorce.

Jenifer paused midway across the Pont Neuf and gazed into the muddy waters of the Seine. She had hated those months away from Duffy. Des Moines had seemed more foreign to her than Paris. She had felt weak, overweight and dismally unattractive. All of her illusions about being the bright-eyed, resourceful mother of three sons had been dissolved by an overwhelming sense of futility. Ed had accused her of being rigid and provincial. Did she really want to spend the rest of her life in Duffy, Iowa, baking cookies and cakes for church bazaars, winning the pie contest at the Warren County fair every fall? Were casseroles and cookies the only things that concerned her? There was nothing subtle in his complaints. She knew he found her boring—a boring housewife with no aspirations.

She paused at an outside café in the heart of St. Germain des Prés on the colorful Left Bank. The aroma of coffee beckoned her. As she sat down at a small table she rehearsed her order in French.

"Un café noir," she told the waiter, *"et un croissant."* Her hands were perspiring and she girded herself for a rebuff from the waiter. Meryl Beamen had warned her that Parisians would be rude and unrelenting where their language was concerned. According to Meryl, Jenifer would be better off if she didn't even bother to try to speak French.

"Merci." The waiter gave her a cordial smile as he turned away and Jen's face relaxed. So far she had received no rebukes for her halting high school French. In any case, she was determined to

11

try to speak. She had unearthed her old French books the day she received word that she would be spending six weeks at Pierre Rennes's Petite Auberge Cooking School. All last summer she had commuted twice a week to the University of Iowa for a crash course.

"Merci bien." Jen blushed as she thanked the waiter, who returned with the cup of steaming black coffee. Every time she opened her mouth to utter even the simplest sentence her face turned scarlet. She felt as if she had "American tourist" engraved in flaming letters on her forehead.

She removed the guidebook from her coat pocket and consulted it. Since she had only one day in Paris before traveling south to Beaune, where the school was located, she wanted to make the most of it. As much as she would have liked to linger in the great city or return perhaps for a weekend later on, such luxuries were not in her budget. The Bradley Bake-off prize included airfare, tuition at the Petite Auberge School and room and board. Any miscellaneous expenses were her responsibility and there were bound to be plenty. Having no financial resources herself, she had borrowed money from her parents, something she had been loath to do, but under the circumstances it had been her only option. If she was ever going to be in the position to support herself and the boys, this was her entrée.

Her brown eyes lit up as she bit into the flaky buttery croissant. Not bad, she thought . . . but I can do it just as well. She closed her eyes, savoring the quality of the roll, analyzing as she always did what was special about it, what might be different or unusual. Cooking . . . food . . . the one area of her life in which she felt absolutely confident.

12

She loved food! She loved to eat it, she loved to cook it!

In the tiny village of Duffy, Iowa, Jenifer Mallory's cooking was revered. Cooking was what she'd done all her life. First there had been pies entered in 4-H, junior baking contests, penny-saving meals she'd whipped up as the eldest of nine children before she'd even married Ed Mallory. There had been courtship cooking . . . extravagant candlelight dinners in the early days of their marriage just after Jen had graduated from high school. Meals for husband, meals for kids—her own and other people's—meals for parents, friends, relatives. Cooking was the one thing she could do, the kitchen the one place she, even in the worst of times, felt confident, creative . . . even powerful.

Of course she'd never thought of it in those analytical terms until the divorce, until she had finally faced the fact that she would never be able to rely on Ed Mallory for anything more than erratic and meager child support. She had finally realized that if she wanted a good life for herself and the boys she was going to have to do it herself—with food. She'd been winning local cooking contests since she was sixteen. It made absolute sense to go for something bigger, and at twenty-seven she had taken the plunge, traveling all the way to Chicago to enter the prestigious Bradley Bake-off. She smiled, remembering the advice the local denizens had given her prior to winning the Bradley contest. In the first place, everyone had wanted to tell her what she should cook. Wisely, she had listened to no one. Secure in her own infallible sense of taste, she had elected to bake a very simple but elegant apple tart.

Meryl Beamen had been appalled by the simplicity of her choice. Even Jen's mother had tried to persuade her to go for something more exotic. But Jen had been right. The Bradley contest had been inundated with exotic gourmet dishes—kiwi mousses, quail stuffed with raisins and artichokes, cold pasta salad with bananas and anchovies. Most contestants approached a divine absurdity in their desperate attempt to be original. Jen's exquisite apple tart was flawless, like a perfectly cut diamond in a sea of garish pretenders.

And she had won! Perhaps now her dream would come true. She would cook for a living. She would begin with a catering business, since she did not have enough money to open a restaurant. But eventually she would gain a reputation that would enable her to get financial backing. In time she would own her own restaurant and inevitably she would succeed.

Jen ordered another cup of the thick coffee and flicked the collar of her coat up around her neck. All around her people were huddled over their morning coffee, reading *Le Figaro* or smoking as they stared absently into the misty day. She ran her hand through her thick carrot-red hair. Normally it fell softly to her shoulders, but because of the dampness in the air she had twisted it into an unruly knot at the nape of her neck. Her face was pale, with a slight sprinkling of light freckles across her slender nose.

She had a wholesome, sturdy look, an openness that immediately identified her as an American. There was a freshness to her scrubbed appearance that brought smiles to the faces of those around her. And it was not just the red hair that was so singularly appealing. There was something infi-

14

nitely likable, solid and even elegant in her salubrious appearance. Although Jenifer herself demurred at the unanimous opinion that she was a remarkably pretty woman, in truth there wasn't a pair of eyes in the Deux Magots Café that had not sent her an admiring glance.

I've never been anywhere, she thought. Outside of the five months spent in Des Moines, the weekend in Chicago, I've spent my entire life in Duffy, Iowa. And I thought it would be so scary. Only it's not. It's just exciting. Meryl Beamen's well-intentioned advice aside, I feel perfectly competent . . . at least as long as I'm eating.

A bubble of laughter rose in her throat. It was true that the only French she felt comfortable with had to do with food. Her years of poring over gourmet magazines and cookbooks had given her a solid understanding of French cooking terms. She would never be thrown by a *poulet, boeuf* or an *aubergine.* She knew her *galantines,* her *charlottes,* her *soufflés* and her *gâteaux.* She was culinarily fluent in French!

Perhaps she would spend the rest of the morning meandering from café to café sampling pastries. The idea made her chuckle out loud. Maybe it was all that caffeine, but something was making her giddy.

Suddenly she was acutely aware of a pair of dark, intensely masculine eyes peering at her over a limp copy of *Le Figaro.* She drew in a quick, embarrassed breath and felt her face turn scarlet. Damn, if only she wasn't cursed with the affliction of blushing, which seemed to go hand in hand with her pale translucent Irish skin and her flaming hair. If she lived to be a hundred she would always be mortified by the intense flush that reddened

15

her cheeks whenever she was embarrassed or uneasy.

Suddenly she felt vulnerable and foolish. She was making a spectacle of herself. As she reached for the check she darted a glance in his direction. He had resumed reading his newspaper. Good. It had probably been her imagination anyway. Maybe this was the way jet lag manifested itself. The heady confidence she had felt moments before was replaced by a jumpiness. Maybe she should take the train to Beaune today, forget about spending a day in Paris. Maybe she should just get settled into her living quarters a day earlier than she'd planned. All at once the idea of walking into one of the fine restaurants alone and ordering dinner was tantamount to jumping off the high diving board at the Warren County Public Pool. And she'd never had the courage to do that.

Who was she kidding anyway? It was one thing to order coffee and a croissant at an outdoor café. It was another to phone ahead for a reservation and carry off the charade at a fancy restaurant. For one thing she knew absolutely nothing about wine. Wouldn't they just laugh if she ordered water?

Jenifer Mallory, she told herself . . . STOP IT! You are in Paris, France, and you're a stupid ninny for sure if you go to a grocery store and buy a cup of yogurt because you're too cowardly to walk into a nice restaurant by yourself. Imagine spending your one night in Paris and eating in your hotel room!

Jen unzipped the new tan leather shoulder bag that Mike's Cub Scout troop had given her for the trip, groping around the odd papers, hairbrush, toothbrush and cosmetic case for the new wallet presented to her by the members of the Methodist choir. A look of panic crossed her face as she searched. The wallet was missing!

Again her face turned scarlet and she had to resist the temptation to dump the contents of the purse onto the table and begin sorting hysterically through the hodgepodge. The wallet was missing!

Both hands stuffed inside the purse, she sat very still, retracing every move she'd made since her arrival. She had not changed her money into francs at the airport. Taking Meryl Beamen's advice, she had waited until she was in the city and then had gone to a Crédit Lyonnaise, where the exchange rates were more favorable. She remembered putting the strange currency into her wallet and then heading for her hotel. She had gone up to her room and . . .

That was it! She was positive the wallet was in her hotel room. She might be naive and she might be terribly excited, but she was not an irresponsible person. If anything, she was overly cautious, and certainly where money was concerned she was extremely prudent. She remembered sitting on the bed in her hotel room, removing her American money from the wallet, putting it into a small zippered bag and placing it in the bottom of her suitcase next to her second booklet of traveler's checks. In her excitement she must have grabbed her purse and gone off, leaving the wallet filled with francs on her bed.

"May I be of any assistance?" The voice was deep and gravelly, and it pierced through the vaporous confusion that clouded her mind. How was it that she knew even before she glanced up that

17

the voice belonged to the same dark eyes that had been staring at her?

"I . . . *J'ai* . . . I have . . ." she stammered between French and English.

"It's all right." He smiled. "I am speaking English to you . . . in case you haven't noticed."

"Oh . . . that's right!" Jen laughed as she met his amused glance.

"You seem to be having a problem."

So she had been making a spectacle of herself after all. She clutched her purse and willed herself to feign a composure she did not feel as she looked at him. His dark eyes sparkled with amusement yet there was a kindness, a softness, in his finely sculpted handsome face.

"I've done something really stupid." She gave an exasperated sigh as she spoke, and his lips trembled slightly as he resisted a smile. There was something in the way he was looking at her that made her feel not so much awkward and naive as . . . warm and even more excited than she had been.

"I just arrived in Paris," she told him in her flat enthusiastic midwestern voice. She met his eyes again and they both laughed. As if she had needed to explain that to him. "I've left my wallet at my hotel." She shrugged apologetically.

"That's no problem." He reached inside his jacket and removed a rich-brown leather wallet. "You only had a coffee and a croissant. Consider me part of your welcoming committee."

"Oh, I couldn't!" Jen blushed and grabbed the check away from him. "I really couldn't let you."

"But what else will you do?"

She gaped at him, trying to draw her eyes away. Had she ever felt herself so swallowed up by such a

18

powerful, dark gaze? And it wasn't just that he was handsome. No, it was more. By any normal standards he was not handsome at all. His head was large and bony, the brows heavy and dark, the nose quite large and dominant, the lips . . . yes, the lips were beautiful indeed. They were very full and perfectly shaped, with a softness that contrasted emphatically with the almost brutal masculinity of his other features.

Staring into those intense eyes, she felt herself even more petite than her five feet two inches. And not only that . . . she felt oddly warm and voluptuous and . . . beautiful. This strange man was gazing at her with open admiration, as if she really were beautiful.

Her pulse thundered inside her head and she heard herself explaining in an amazingly calm voice that she had left her money in her hotel room, that it wasn't as if she were in serious trouble.

"All the same . . ." He withdrew a bill from his wallet and placed it on the table.

"That's very nice of you," Jen jumped in, "but my hotel isn't far. Just across the river . . . maybe a twenty-minute walk only. I'll just hurry on over and come back with the money."

"I see." He nodded and this time his amused attitude made her uneasy.

"If you could just explain to the waiter," she went on. "My French is very elementary. If you could tell him I'll be back as quickly as I can."

This time he laughed full out, a great, low rumbling laugh that filled his entire body. *"Pardonnezmoi, Madame,* I am so sorry to laugh, but do you really expect a Parisian waiter to accept such an explanation?"

How naive could a person be? Jen stood up abruptly, feeling her Irish temper begin to flare, feeling so ridiculously small-town foolish that she could have fled.

"I suppose you're right," she admitted tightly.

"I am right." He touched her elbow lightly and a myriad of dazzling sensations flooded in on her. Anger and humiliation dissolved as her body was charged with an onslaught of erotic currents. What was happening?

"Jet lag," she muttered dazedly after he had paid the waiter and stood waiting for his change. Maybe all of the crazy wild flutterings were just another manifestation of jet lag. If only she had listened to Meryl Beamen.

"I beg your pardon?" He leaned down attentively. Now that she was standing next to him, she felt even more acutely the sensual power of his massive form.

"I said . . . jet lag." She threw him a vague smile. "I must be suffering from jet lag. I'm not the sort of person who goes off leaving her purse in a hotel room."

"I'm glad you did." He smiled softly, and she was completely thrown off guard by the gentle simplicity of his reply.

"But I'm going to pay you back," she told him as they walked back out onto the boulevard. "I could mail you the money, or if you have the time I could pay you back immediately. Like I said . . . my hotel is just across the Seine . . . near the Louvre. I'm afraid I don't know the name of the street, but I swear to you . . . I know exactly how to get there." She glanced up at his austere Gallic profile and laughed suddenly. "You must think I'm just an absolute . . . dingbat."

"Dingbat?" He gave her a curious look.

"A dingbat!" She laughed harder, whether from nerves, frustration or jet lag, she did not know. "A dingbat is American slang for someone who has very little mental capacity. Someone who is all fluff, shallow . . . not to be taken seriously."

"I should like to take you seriously." He gave her a flirtatious smile.

She ignored the innuendo but her stomach was twirling, and beneath the navy raincoat, beneath the brown wool dress she was wearing, her body tingled with a desire that took her completely by surprise.

He slipped his arm through hers as they turned onto the Rue Bonaparte. She was speechless, aware only of the deep erotic sensations his touch had ignited.

"I'm . . . Jenifer Mallory." She felt mesmerized by the sensation of his strong muscular arm guiding her.

He stopped walking suddenly and looked at her. "Jenifer Mallory." He repeated her name.

The sound of his deep voice, with its thick French accent intoning her name, sent shivers up her spine.

"You are cold?" He put a protective hand around her shoulder.

"No, no . . ." Jen seized the opportunity to put some distance between them. She removed her arm, sashed her raincoat more tightly at the waist and turned up her collar against the wind.

"You just arrived?" He studied her as they walked along.

"Yes. Just this morning. I've been walking ever since."

"You should dress more warmly." Even though

21

they were no longer touching, she still felt the power of his virile body.

"Jenifer Mallory," he said again. "I like it," he announced, and his face took on a crinkly warmth that was altogether disarming. "It's a very wholesome name. A little bit like apple pie."

"I suppose it is." Jen grinned, falling into stride beside him.

"Is it Irish?"

"Irish and Welsh, with some Dutch thrown in on my mother's side of the family."

"And there are no sneaky French influences?"

"Why sneaky?" Jen glanced at him. Reading the devilish look in his dark eyes, she laughed again with the almost giddy pleasure of partaking in such a zany conversation. Back at the café he had appeared so dark, mysterious and formidable. The lightness and buoyancy of his humor took her completely by surprise.

"I don't know why sneaky," he chuckled. "Of course, the English think we're sneaky . . . or maybe that's putting it too nicely. They think we are absolute scoundrels! By the way, did you know that the French actually invaded Ireland, briefly? That there was an underground revolutionary movement in Ireland and their ally was France?"

"You're a historian?" Jen queried.

"I'm a dabbler in historic trivia," he admitted. "Although I've often imagined myself, in my later years, buried under volumes of history books. I find it all fascinating."

"I know what you mean." Jen nodded. To her surprise she was not self-conscious with him, as she had been with so many men since her divorce. Usually she felt so ill at ease with men, even unworthy. Having been rejected by one man, she felt she would most certainly be rejected again. And yet here she was having a lovely time with this French stranger, a man who seemed so interested, so happy to be with her.

It came as quite a surprise to her. As they continued their walk she thought of how little happiness she had had in the past year, how accustomed she had become to living without it. Returning to Duffy to live with her parents and care for the boys had demanded all of her energies, and she had hardly had time for herself. She had always thought of herself as someone who didn't want much, a woman who was easily satisfied with what little she had. Until she'd hit upon the idea of using her greatest talent, cooking, as a way to get more out of her life. From that moment the future appeared bright. From that moment she had been seized with a real desire all her own, to do something with her life, to do something for herself. Finally she understood that she was a woman of strong and varied appetites.

But until this moment she had never considered that those appetites might include a man.

CHAPTER TWO

His name was Robert Pierre and they spent the rest of the morning sight-seeing. It was silly to be swept away by the romance of the moment, but when they stood together on top of Notre-Dame gazing down at the gracefully curving Seine, the beauty of the scene brought tears to her eyes.

Along their walk they visited a lovely sculpture museum located in an elegant old residence, something she would never have known to do on her own. It was the Hôtel Biron, Robert explained, one of the grand Faubourg homes that had been converted into a museum.

"It's almost too beautiful out here to go inside," Jen said, fingering the velvety petals of a red rose in the garden outside the museum.

"Yes." Robert smiled, enjoying her appreciation. "I think that much sculpture is shown to best advantage outside. Especially the Rodins . . . the large pieces."

"I have a confession," Jen said as they mounted the steps to the Hôtel Biron.

"What is that?" He looked at her intently.

"I have never been to a sculpture museum," Jen admitted, not feeling the least bit embarrassed by her confession.

"But that is wonderful." He smiled. "It is wonderful to have so much to look forward to, so many new experiences to enjoy for the first time. And I have a confession as well," he told her with an impish grin. "I have never been on a horse. And oddly enough it is something that concerns me, from time to time. Do you understand? I mean, it is a . . . fantasy, if you will, to ride like one of your Western cowboys."

"Not everybody in the U.S.A. rides like that," Jen assured him with a smile.

"Exactly." Robert nodded. "It must take a great deal of skill. In any case, I would not like you to get the wrong impression that I spend a lot of hours daydreaming about galloping across the prairie. But it is something I would like to try."

"No, I know what you mean." Jen smiled. "Well, you should try it."

"There never seems to be time," he admitted.

"I guess that's why I never made it to a sculpture museum until now," Jen reflected.

"Well, it is my honor to be your escort." Robert held the door to the museum itself open for her. "And this is my favorite. It is my fortune that you forgot your change purse and I had a business meeting canceled this morning."

It is my fortune, too, Jen thought as she studied a large statue of Victor Hugo. Robert was a delightful guide, speaking fondly of several pieces of sculpture as if they were old friends.

He was vague about his business but she knew he was important. There was an air of decisiveness

25

in everything he did, as if he were accustomed to giving orders. And yet, at the same time, there seemed to be something artistic in his nature.

Back in her hotel room, Jenifer stood in front of the clouded oval-shaped mirror and stared at herself standing limp-armed in her worn white nylon slip. Her red hair was frizzed and unruly from the misty day. She sucked in her stomach and turned sideways, frowning at her ample hips, which would never please her no matter how much weight she lost. She would never have boyish hips like those sunken-cheeked fashion models on the covers of *Vogue.* From the squiggles of her unruly hair to the tips of her tiny pink toes she was all curves. An hourglass figure, Meryl Beamen liked to say, and maybe it was true. But even if it was, Jenifer wasn't impressed with it.

As she stared at herself she wondered what a man like Robert Pierre had seen in her. Why had he spent an entire morning with her? Why had he seemed so interested in her life in Duffy, her sons, her parents' farm and the first prize she'd won in the Bradley Bake-off? Her life in Duffy was so far from being glamorous as to be ludicrous. And then he had asked her to dinner. Why would he do a thing like that?

Jen padded over to her bed and flopped down on her back with a sigh. She was utterly exhausted. Jet lag.

The world seemed fuzzy and she felt a bit queasy. Yet her heart was pounding like crazy and every time she thought of Robert Pierre her body was racked with desire.

Desire. That was a word she had almost forgotten. Lately, it was a word she read in books, a word which for many years had not applied to her. She

26

and Ed had married because that was the thing to do. They had known each other for years and never fought. They were both mild-mannered people. Everyone in Duffy had said they were made for each other. But there had been little passion between them.

Jen closed her eyes and Robert Pierre's broad shoulders floated in her mind's eye. His tweed suit had been of the finest cut. His shoes, like his brown leather wallet, were clearly the best. Once, as they sat on a bench in the Tuileries breathing in the deep wet green of the trees, he lit a slender brown cigarette, which he had withdrawn from a beautiful gold case.

"A bad habit." He had smiled, his dark eyes crinkling, narrowing almost to slits. "Most Frenchmen would not admit that smoking is anything but sexy . . . that, like love, it can be hazardous. Yes, we Frenchmen are stubborn to the very end. We like our traditions and we have a weakness . . . for cigarettes and love."

He had looked off and Jen had sensed a bitterness in him. For several moments he had been silent, remote, as if he had forgotten she was there.

She had the impression that he was a complex man, a man of many moods, perhaps even an unhappy man. Large and well-built, he was a powerful, rather intimidating figure. But though she had from time to time that morning felt an aloofness, a sternness and preciseness, in him which might manifest itself in temperament, there was nothing brutal in his nature. It had been his idea to sit in the hushed verdant depths of the Tuileries and he had been content to drink in the silence.

Sitting in a park, in silence, with a man was something else she'd never done before. Jen racked her mind to think of any man she had ever met—uncle, brother, friend, acquaintance—whom she could imagine sitting in a park with . . . just listening to the twitter of birds. Allowing the silence to pour into him . . . was how Robert Pierre had put it. Occasionally his manner of speech had seemed almost like poetry. Not that she'd read that much poetry, but his speech was different from that of most of the men she knew. Well, perhaps it was because his native tongue was French, a far more poetic language than her own.

Most of the men she knew talked very little. The only conversations she could remember having with Ed were centered around problems. What movie would they see that night? Who could they call to baby-sit? What could they do to get Mike to stop bullying Timmy, etc., etc.

Jen rolled over onto her stomach and buried her head in the pillow. She really should get some sleep. Robert had business meetings all afternoon but was stopping by for her around six so they could have a drink at the Eiffel Tower before going to dinner.

She sat up suddenly, her pulse racing, her brown eyes damp with anticipation. For an instant the breath seemed to catch in her throat. She fled into the tiled bathroom, filled a glass with water and sat on the edge of the oversized tub drinking it. She had to get hold of herself!

She gulped down another glass of water. Yes, she had better get used to the idea that her encounter with Robert Pierre was just a nice romantic adventure that would be concluded this evening when he dropped her at the hotel after dinner. Why was she allowing herself to get all het up? Her reasons for coming to France had nothing to do with pleasure. She was here strictly on business. In fact, it would be wise for her to consider her dinner with him business. She had wanted to dine at a fine restaurant, to sample the famed *haute cuisine,* and Robert's presence would make everything easier. But it would be business and she would tell him so from the start. She would insist on paying her share so there would be no mistake!

"I don't like to argue with you, Jenifer." Robert Pierre's dark eyes regarded her as they sat across from each other at dinner that evening. They were at a small table, beautifully set with a pale pink cloth, large white damask napkins, gleaming silver, tall-stemmed wine goblets and china plates ringed in gold. Relais Louis XV was a minuscule restaurant tucked in an alley down a remote cobblestone street on the Rive Gauche. It was a former *cave,* a stone wine cellar, attached to a nearby mansion. The low vaulted ceilings and Gothic arched doorways lent a mysterious medieval ambience to the elegant flower-filled restaurant. Here, as earlier in the park, the silence that enveloped them seemed timeless, magical.

"Look." He reached across the table and took her hand, lavishing another admiring look into her eyes as he had done throughout their evening. "I invited you. You are my guest."

"But I told you, Robert. This is a new beginning for me. You've already done so many things for me today. I feel like I really got to know Paris because of you. I know for sure I want to come back."

"I'm sure you will." Robert smiled.

Jen withdrew her hand and fastened her eyes on the velvety petals of the pale pink roses as she spoke. "You see, I'm not used to thinking of myself as . . . as a person who has to make decisions and

29

. . . accomplish things. In a business sense. I want to learn all I can about food . . . about the specifics of running a restaurant, about ambience and all the gracious details which contribute to the overall effect."

"I didn't realize this was a business dinner." Robert raised one of his thick black eyebrows and for an instant Jen thought he was annoyed.

Then he smiled and, lifting his wineglass, toasted her with his amber-filled goblet. "To you, Jenifer. To your success. From what you've told me about Duffy, Iowa, I should say you are destined to succeed."

Jen leaned across the table, heady from the wine. "You have to understand that it isn't easy for me to . . . to even broach the subject of . . . money. All my life . . . when something bothers me I've just kept quiet about it."

She felt her cheeks stinging red again, but this time, perhaps because of the wine but also because of the company, she was not embarrassed. She was exhilarated! Her ability to articulate her honest concerns to him was another first. And it had been so much easier than she'd anticipated. In fact, everything seemed easy with him. She couldn't get over the way he seemed to hang on her every word, probing for details, asking for more instead of cutting her off to launch into a story centering on himself.

Jen reached for her wine goblet, aware of his warm, appreciative gaze. She'd agonized over what to wear that evening and had ended up choosing a black sleeveless sweater with a plunging V neckline and a plain straight-cut black skirt. Her hair, still a mass of unruly ringlets, was pulled back behind her ears and held in place with two tiny gold barrettes. She wore no jewelry save a pair of small round gold earrings.

"I don't mean to make a big thing out of having to make business decisions." She paused with the goblet touching her lips.

"You're not," Robert assured her. "I think I understand . . . where . . . you're coming from. Isn't that how they say it in English . . . where you're coming from?"

Jen gave an irrepressible laugh. He spoke English with such formality that his use of slang was incongruous.

"I suppose that's what they say in Los Angeles or New York," she said. "In Duffy nobody much talks about 'where you're coming from.' "

"Duffy is not a racy town?"

Jen laughed again. "Duffy is the last of the one-horse towns. Do you understand 'one-horse town'?"

"I've seen a lot of American movies," Robert nodded. "So tell me, Jenifer . . ."

"It's okay then?" Jen interrupted.

"You know this is most unusual," Robert teased her lightly. "I could have taken you to a restaurant where they don't even print the price of dinners on the menus they give to the lady."

"They don't put the price on the menu?" Jen blinked in astonishment.

"Only on the menus that are given to the men. It's an old custom and it prevails in many of the finest restaurants in France. Tour d'Argent, I'm certain, still adheres to the old tradition, and I'm not sure if Lasserre has adopted a more egalitarian policy or not. I suppose it's fortuitous that I've happened to bring you to a restaurant that does include prices for both sexes."

"I've never heard of such a thing." Jen shook her head.

"It was assumed that the lady should not worry her pretty little head over such a nasty thing as money." Robert's deep voice held a touch of bitterness.

"But that's exactly my point." Jen gave him an earnest look.

"I understand that it is."

"So it's settled, then?" Jen was amazed at her persistence in the matter. Robert Pierre was more dignified, handsome and sophisticated than any man she had ever known. Yet, incredibly, she was able to stand up to him, to speak her thoughts to him more easily than with anyone else.

"A compromise?" Robert raised a thick eyebrow and there was a devilish glint in his eye.

"No compromise." Jen laughed.

"We split the dinner but I treat you to the wine. After all, I've noticed I tend to imbibe considerably more than you."

"That's fair." She grinned. "They'd never get away with it in the United States, you know."

"You mean leaving the prices off of a woman's menu?"

"You wouldn't know how much anything cost! Wouldn't know if you were ordering the most expensive thing on the menu and . . ."

"Women aren't supposed to care about that sort of thing."

Jen looked up abruptly at the cruel note which crept into his voice.

"But if the information's always been withheld, how are they supposed to learn to be responsible?" Jen countered.

32

"Are you one of those feminists we hear so much about over here?" he chided her.

Jen laughed heartily this time and the tightness that had clouded his face disappeared as he watched her. "Oh, no! Hardly. I mean, I never think of it . . . or never did until after my divorce. I just went along with things. I did whatever Ed thought was right and never thought anything about it. I was too busy with the boys to do too much thinking."

"Your former husband made all the decisions, did he?"

"Except in the kitchen." She grinned. "Ed prided himself on not being able to boil an egg. I must admit I was glad he couldn't. Imagine what a mess I'd be in if I hadn't been good at something. I could always wow him with some rich dessert. At least . . . almost always. For a long time it seemed to be true that the way to a man's heart is through his stomach."

"And you're really not bitter, are you?"

Jen shook her head and smiled softly. No, she really wasn't bitter. Shortly after returning to her parents' farm with the boys she knew that Ed's decision to leave her was the best thing for her, for everyone . . . even for the boys. After the initial ego-shattering realization that she had failed, it finally dawned on her that she had been numb to her own unhappiness, living in the cramped little house in Des Moines.

"I know there'll be times during the next six weeks when I'll be so homesick for my boys I'll probably think this is the dumbest move I've ever made. But I know I've done the right thing. It's the first time in my life I've ever taken the reins in my own hands."

33

"You seem an expert to me." Robert nudged her lightly under the table with his knee. The innocent, friendly gesture sent a hot current through her.

"I bet you were in the driver's seat more than you realized," he observed.

"Maybe." Jen shifted uneasily in her chair and wished the waiter would bring their entrées. It was too easy talking to him, too easy to give in to the rich sensuality of the evening. She was keenly aware of his long legs beneath the table, too intrigued by how his soft full lips would feel opening slowly onto hers. She vowed to have nothing more to drink, but in the fecund silence that followed she reached for her wine goblet out of nervousness. Robert's fascination for the details of her life, details which seemed mundane and just the slightest bit boring to her, made her wary.

The silence in the old *cave* seemed to absorb every sound except the pounding of her own heart. She avoided his eyes as a suave waiter placed their plates before them.

"Oh . . . this looks . . ." Jen could not contain her enthusiasm as she looked at the *caneton braisé aux marrons* (braised duck with chestnut and sausage stuffing), which was surrounded by the crispest and slenderest of shoestring potatoes.

"And yours . . ." Her eyes flew open at the sight of Robert's delicate fish filets, which had been poached in white wine and were served with a velvety cream sauce.

"Is it a *velouté?*" she asked after she had savored her own meaty duck. "The sauce, I mean. Is it a simple *velouté* or has it a bit of cheese in it?"

Robert's craggy face broke into a wide grin. "I

see now that you are a true cook, a born eater. You are angling for a taste of my fish, no?"

Jen nodded, laughing. "I was tempted to order it myself, only because I knew I'd want to try it. I can't stand not having a taste of anything I lay my eyes on."

Robert gave her a brief scorching look, which ignited her in ways she had never imagined possible.

"A *velouté* is generally made just from the fish poaching liquid and a roux . . . a butter and flour mixture." She covered her reaction with a hurried explanation of the cooking term.

"I think there is a trifle bit of cheese in it." Robert offered her a morsel on the prong of his fork and as Jen opened her mouth he slipped it inside.

Her heart was galloping wildly, and even though she was seated she had the sense that she might collapse. She did not dare look into his eyes as she chewed the moist white fish. She reached for her glass of wine and felt his eyes caressing her throat as she swallowed. Despite her efforts to concentrate on the duck, she could not rid herself of the sensation of his long muscular fingers pressing into her torso, drawing her closer.

Each intoxicating flavor stirred some long dormant passion deep within her. After so much talk they had both grown silent, but it was a highly charged erotic silence. As they ate it seemed to grow more demanding and intense.

"Superb." She tried to flash him a light, composed smile and was stunned to see in his dark eyes the same moist hunger that had overtaken her.

"Formidable." Was it her imagination or did he seem to be as stunned as she was by what was

35

happening between them. Suddenly they could neither look at each other nor say a word. It was as if the slightest connection might set off a chain reaction of volatile explosives.

"It's three in the afternoon in Duffy," she said, shying away from him when they finally left the restaurant and walked out into the crisp night air. She wanted to put space between them to stop the wild ricocheting sensations.

"I'm catching an early train to Dijon tomorrow morning. I can't miss it. Someone must drive up from Beaune to meet me . . . it's not far, I understand. So . . . I really should go straight back to my hotel, Robert. I don't want to take you out of your way. If I could just get a cab . . ."

"I'm seeing you back to your hotel." Robert's low voice stirred another onslaught of desire. When he took her arm she felt her body grow supple with a warm eagerness that made her sway against him.

How quickly he sensed her slightest acquiescence. Wrapping his arms around her, he molded her full against his virile body. She could not think. His hardness obliterated everything and she melted against him in the flickering shadows of the street.

It seemed almost as if she could taste him and that he was robust and rich, sweet and velvety, pungent, bitter. . . . His arms tightened around her. His overcoat was open and he shifted so that she was enclosed inside the soft cashmere fabric. Her face was turned sideways against the nubby tweed of his jacket. His heart thudded against her cheekbone and she held her breath, suspended.

He made no move and neither did she, though she knew something stirred deeply in him as it did in her. They clung together cloaked in passion, cauterized by the intimacy of the moment.

"I want you." His breath was warm inside her ear. Her breasts tingled at his words. No man had ever said that to her before.

Nothing like this day had ever happened to her. Perhaps nothing so romantic and stimulating would ever happen to her again. Maybe she should seize the moment. For just an instant it occurred to her that anything was possible. After all, she would never see him again.

She squeezed her eyes shut, tightening her arms around his broad back and clenching her fingers into fists. She was quickly losing control. What would they think back home? One night away on her own and look what was happening.

Only no one would ever know.

A lover . . . she might have a lover. The word alone triggered an erotic convulsion. A lover? She was not the sort of woman to have a lover! She was Jenifer Mallory, steady, reliable mother of three, a good egg, shy and likable . . . the sort of woman other women and Cub Scouts love. But not the sort of woman to take a lover!

But even if it was only for one night . . . she would have a lover.

"You are right, of course!" He stepped out of the embrace abruptly. "You are absolutely right. You must go directly to your hotel!"

Jen stared at him, shocked at his sudden change of heart.

He took her arm firmly and they walked briskly and silently out to the Boulevard St. Michel, where he succeeded in locating a taxi cab. Inside the cab he sat with his arms folded, a truculent, almost angry expression on his face. Jen watched him out of the corner of her eye, her heart still racing from the delicious sensations of his body against hers.

"Sorry," he said curtly without looking at her.

"That's all right." Jen threw him a concerned look. She wanted to reach out and touch his hand, to soothe and comfort him. Yet she had no idea what had thrust him into such a morose state.

"It's just that I am not so forgiving as you," he said in a low whisper as the cab veered around the Place de la Concorde.

"I don't understand," Jen said.

"I am bitter about my divorce."

"I didn't know . . ."

"Of course you didn't!" he snapped. "I didn't mention it. I'm sorry. This is a hell of a way to end an enjoyable evening. I am truly sorry to inflict my . . . please, will you forgive me?"

Jen nodded mutely. She told herself that perhaps this was for the best. Now that she understood he was recently divorced, his behavior over the course of the day made absolute sense. He had been alone in Paris. He had been lonely and needed companionship. It was that simple.

Touched by his sadness, Jen leaned over and, without thinking, gently brushed her lips against the stubble of his left cheek.

"Good night, Robert," she said. She could not have known the stirring mixture of regret and passion which colored her pale face as she stepped from the cab out onto the dark street.

38

CHAPTER THREE

Of course she wouldn't see him again. It was foolish to think otherwise. Back inside her hotel room, Jen paced from the bureau to the bed with a catlike frustration which was entirely foreign to her.

"Jet lag," she muttered as she undressed and laid out the clothes she would wear when she left early the next morning. Still, she could not rid herself of the hot delicious sensation which had swept over her when he had pressed tight against her. She fought off imagining what it would have been like to feel his mouth on hers. So far Meryl Beamen's advice had been useless. Jen should have been warned about Frenchmen instead of jet lag!

The next morning she dressed in a pleated gray wool skirt and a lavender sweater that accentuated her delicate pale skin and made her red hair even more vivid. But Jenifer didn't see it that way. Entering the *boulangerie* to buy a *bagette* to eat on the train, she felt painfully unfashionable. Like an aging junior miss, she thought as she jammed her change into her wallet and hurried back out onto the boulevard. A woman walking ahead of her was smartly dressed in a voluminous black cape and high tan leather boots. Even the older, middle-aged women in their conservative tweed suits and sensible shoes had an air of finesse and style about them.

And what was she wearing? A skirt left over from college that hit her mid-calf. And as far as she could see, that was the *only* length that was inappropriate at the moment.

Damn, she was feeling irritable and unsettled. Despite the sunny day, she was fraught with feelings of misgiving. It was not even morning back in Duffy. The boys would still be sound asleep in their beds.

She paid her hotel bill and climbed into the waiting cab, which deposited her in front of the Gare de Lyon. As she was struggling to remove the two huge suitcases from the cab, someone called to her.

"Robert?" She dropped the suitcases and gaped at him as he leaped out from behind the wheel of a yellow Citroën convertible to intercept her.

"I've been waiting here for an hour." He swept both of her suitcases under one arm and steered her toward his car with the other. "I thought you said you were taking the *early* train."

"What are you doing here?" Jenifer looked as if she had seen a ghost.

"Nothing against the French National Railroad," he laughed, "but it's too fine a day to be cooped up inside a train. I stopped at Fauchon and had them make up a picnic lunch. My business plans for the day were canceled, and since I found myself on the way to Lyon, it occurred to me that you might join me."

"I'm . . . I'm going to Beaune," Jenifer stammered as he helped her into the passenger seat. His hand lingered momentarily on her elbow and she averted her eyes from his face.

"I know you're going to Beaune. Could I have forgotten? But Lyon is just to the south. I assure you, you will not be taking me out of my way."

All of the startling warm sensations which had swept over her last night flooded in on her with renewed vigor. She did not believe his story.

With a combined sense of exhilaration and trepidation she watched him slip the key into the ignition. He was wearing the same nubby tweed jacket he had worn last night, only today he wore a black turtleneck sweater underneath instead of a shirt and tie. Her stomach lurched in remembrance of the scratchy texture of the wool against her cheek.

"Robert, I . . ."

"No, no, no!" He covered her mouth gently with one hand, silencing her. The sensation of her lips against the flat of his palm made her flush. "You mustn't protest! Today is a rare day, do you know that? Do you know how unusual it is for the sun to shine in Paris? And that means it will be dazzling in the country . . . and it is in the country that you will truly learn to love France."

He removed his hand and gave her a long searching look as he maneuvered the Citroën through rush traffic. Why are you going to Lyon? Jenifer wondered. Do you live in Lyon? Who are you? Jenifer could not hide her skepticism but she said nothing. By the time they were speeding along the highway she had relaxed somewhat in her suspicions. There was a definite ambiguity in his manner that was even more pronounced today than it had been yesterday. But the truth was, she was flattered. If he was lying about something, it was because he wanted to be with her.

Wanted to be with her . . . She surrendered to the idea of being . . . desired. It was a wonderful experience. The wind whipped at her hair as they drove. Her tiny face was practically obscured in a tangle of red curls. She smoothed it back with both hands and glanced at him at precisely the same moment that he turned his eyes away from the road to look at her. His dark eyes crinkled in a seductive smile and he laughed, reaching for her hand and squeezing it warmly. There was a robust friendliness in his attitude toward her, as if he had known her for a long time and was welcoming her home.

It was as if he had turned a key in her. She tossed her head back, laughing with him, laughing for no particular reason except for the sheer pleasure of sitting next to him as they sped along under a cloudless sky.

"The sky!" he shouted above the roar of the engine, and Jen leaned back with her head on the seat, staring up into the unbroken expanse of brilliant blue. She couldn't remember the last time she'd felt so happy and so alive. If only the feeling could last. She closed her eyes, feeling the warmth of the sun, the wind and the speed. Pierre drove extremely fast, but then she'd noticed in Paris that automotive speed was a national affliction. She smiled softly, enjoying the wild sensation.

If only it didn't have to end. If only Robert could be a part of her life during the next six weeks. Well, perhaps he could visit. . . . Her mouth tightened and she checked herself. This was not a vacation. Still . . . it would be nice to have her cake and eat it too!

She fell into a delicious sleep, so much better than last night's fitful tossing about. The Citroën motion lulled her deeper and deeper into a state of relaxation. At the same time she was keenly aware of her surroundings. Several times she felt the car slow to near stopping, then pick up speed again. Once it seemed to her that Robert was humming softly in his rich deep baritone. But she was suspended, content to luxuriate in the wonder of this unique experience.

"Ma chère," Robert leaned over and whispered into her ear and she opened her eyes lazily. It seemed perfectly natural to be awakened by him on some strange country road.

"Up there . . ." He pointed to some old stone towers in the distance. "Chambertin . . . one of the oldest villages in Burgundy. This is where the Côte d'Or commences. Each village is like a trip into the distant past. Many of these domains have existed for centuries, many are still owned and managed by the same family."

Jenifer twisted around in her seat marveling at the soft, muted beauty of the fields, which were planted with the most renowned grapes in the world.

"I have a confession." She turned to him. "Of course I've heard of the Côte d'Or. But I've never tasted one of the great wines from the region."

"Then we shall remedy that!" Robert shifted smoothly into gear and the Citroën shot back onto the highway.

Minutes later he turned off the highway and

43

began driving up into the rich green hills that overlooked the flat stretch of vineyards below.

"Look how they've mulched the vines with rocks!" Jen leaned far out over the side of the car.

"Careful." Robert tugged at her waist and she plopped back down onto the seat, laughing.

"What a sleep I had!" she cried. "What a dreadful, boring companion I turned out to be."

"I was flattered." Robert threw her a smile.

"Flattered because I fell asleep?"

"Because you felt comfortable enough to take the sleep you needed so badly. I've been accused of being something of a . . . how do you say? Ah yes . . . a speed demon."

"Well, I would never accuse you of being a slow poke," Jen laughed. "Most of the time I felt as if I were flying!"

They wound higher and higher into the hills until they were quite suddenly in the center of a tiny, ancient village.

"Musigny," Robert announced fondly as he halted the car to allow a horse-drawn wagon piled high with weathered wooden barrels to pass.

"It's a bit early for the *vendanges* . . . that's what they call the final harvesting of the grapes. It's a wild, joyous time. In another month the grapes will be ripe and the fields will be alive with the songs of pickers and the smell of grapes will fill the autumn air. There is no better time to be in Burgundy."

Jenifer stared at an old stone church in the center of the little town. The streets were cobblestone, the houses all made of stone. A sense of timeless dignity pervaded the sleepy village.

Robert turned off the main square and down a slight incline, stopping in front of a wide bronzed gate. He jumped out of the car and ran around to open her door.

"We'll pick up a bottle of my favorite Musigny," he said.

"Ah, Pierre!" The gate opened and they were warmly greeted by a crusty old frenchman.

"Just a bottle, Jacques." Robert pounded the old man on the back as they embraced. "The '76 would be nice."

Jenifer was straining to keep up with the rapid barrage of french.

"Jacques"—he spoke very slowly in French for Jenifer's benefit—"this is an American friend of mine, Madame Jenifer Mallory."

Jenifer stifled a laugh as she clasped the old man's hand. Madame Mallory! How her sons would hoot if they heard that. Madame Mallory of Duffy, Iowa!

Robert put his hand lightly on her shoulder as they waited for Jacques to return with the bottle of wine.

"*Merci.*" Robert handed Jacques a wad of money but the old man shook his head vehemently and waved them both off.

"He likes you," Jen observed as Robert climbed behind the wheel again.

"He never lets me pay when I stop by the estate." Robert shook his head.

"How do you know him?" Jen inquired.

"I've known the family for years," Robert said quickly, and something guarded in his tone made her uneasy.

"Why did he call you Pierre and not Robert?"

Robert darted a quick look in her direction and his mouth tightened. "A joke. Do you not sometimes do the same thing with close friends in your

45

country? I mean, don't you sometimes call a person by his last name . . . almost as a sign of affection."

"Oh, yes." Jen nodded. She was so busy glancing at the sights around her, she scarcely heard the tension in his voice.

However, once they were settled under a leafy bower next to a huge stone ledge overlooking the villages below, his ebullient mood returned. Robert uncorked the bottle of Burgundy and poured the wine into the two small silver chalices he withdrew from the picnic hamper.

"You come prepared!" Jen accepted the chalice with a smile. She already felt giddy. No telling what might happen after a glass or two of wine.

"I do come prepared." Robert grinned and began laying out the spectacular array of delicacies.

"Compliments of Fauchon." Robert handed her a slice of *pâté en croute.*

Jen gasped as he presented her with a box filled with assorted pastries. "Oh, I'm going to get *soooo* fat." She popped a tiny tart into her mouth and met his eyes, laughing.

"A raspberry tart for an hors d'oeuvre. You must think I'm terribly *déclassé!"*

"I think," Robert looked deeply into her eyes, "you are the most spectacular woman I have ever met."

His compliment shook her so deeply that she did not even blush. She felt herself spiraling into the singular, overwhelming warmth of his gaze. She could not tear her eyes away, and for what seemed an eternity their eyes locked in a look of shattering sensuality.

"Taste . . ." Before she could recover Robert touched his silver goblet to her parted lips.

Jen lowered her eyes to the deep Burgundy, inhaling its heavy ripe aroma. The scent alone was like some rare aphrodisiac.

"They call this a feminine wine," Robert said softly as she swallowed. "It is round and soft, voluptuous and yielding."

Jen drew in a deep breath and helped herself to a tiny black olive. "And are there masculine wines too?"

"But of course." Robert broke the spellbinding moment with a low laugh. "Chambertin is a masculine wine. Sometime perhaps we will compare them. With your highly developed palate you will have no difficulty discerning the difference."

"I know this is good." Jen took another sip, this time from her own goblet. "The only wine I've had other than the nice wine you bought last night at dinner was a very inexpensive California wine. It went down fast. This goes down slow."

"You see," Robert chuckled, "you are already a connoisseur! Actually they are making excellent wines in the United States these days. If the French do not watch their step, they will lose their edge on the market."

"What do you do, Robert?" Jen asked suddenly. "I mean, besides drink wine and go on picnics."

"I am in business," Robert tore off a hunk of bread and put a slab of cheese on it before handing it to her.

"Yes, but what kind of business?" Jen laughed as he stuffed it into her mouth.

"Now, Jenifer, last night you insisted it was business. Today I insist that it is not."

Jenifer nodded as she chewed. He was being evasive, but so what. She would not think about that. She would seize the moment for what it was.

"You understand?" he felt a need to justify his reticence. "Sometimes I want just to forget about business. Don't you think it dominates too much of life sometimes? Isn't it good just to abandon everything occasionally and surrender to the sun and the lingering taste of the wine?"

Yes, it was good to surrender. Jen cut into a slender slice of what looked like pâté and popped it into her mouth. The morsel, which was like nothing she had ever before tasted, melted almost instantly.

"Foie gras." Robert was enjoying her reactions to the varied tastes.

"Oh!" Jen's dark eyes twinkled as she looked at him. There was no need telling him she had never tasted the rare delicacy before. He already knew.

She stretched her legs out and leaned back on her elbows. It was odd that he seemed to know so much about her, that he seemed instinctively to understand what would bring her pleasure. For instance, this day, being outside, sitting on a hillside with the midday sun beating down. How could he have known that out of all the options in life, this was perhaps the one she most enjoyed?

"May I compliment you again?" he asked after a moment.

"Please." Jen laughed. "I'm so bad at accepting compliments!"

"I'm going to do it anyway." He nudged her shoe with the tip of his. "It is such a treat to be with you. I mean it. You are very different from the French women I know."

Jen shook her head, thinking how unfashionable she had felt that morning in Paris. She had felt downright dowdy and now . . . under Robert's gaze she felt almost beautiful.

"You are so open, so friendly, so free from subterfuge."

"Subterfuge?" Jen sat forward and helped herself to another morsel of *foie gras*.

"I mean, you do not seem to enjoy a game, as so many women do."

Jen looked at him seriously. "Is it possible you're speaking from your own hurt?"

Now what on earth had prompted her to say that? She held her breath, certain that her candor had offended him. It wasn't like her to speak her mind with such ease. And after the bitterness he had expressed last night? How tactless of her.

"It is possible," he admitted after a moment.

"Well"—Jen sprang to her knees and dipped her hand into the pastry box, anxious to steer the conversation back onto a lighter plane—"since you're forcing me to indulge in another sinful sweet."

"Tell me about your sons." Robert stretched out on his stomach with his chin resting on his hands. "You hardly seem old enough to be the mother of three boys."

"My nine-year-old, Mike, is almost as tall as I am." Jen's dark eyes sparkled as she talked. "I had him when I was eighteen and two years later Timmy was born and one year later . . . David."

"You were very busy," Robert observed wryly.

"Anyway, they're all wonderful boys . . . impossible, rowdy, demanding and . . . and if I don't stop talking about them I'm going to cry."

"No, no," Robert reached out and touched her cheek tenderly. "I can see that it must have been a difficult decision leaving them. But you mustn't worry. The separation will be good for them as it will be good for you."

"I hope so." Jen allowed him to refill her wineglass.

"Oh, it will!" His eyes scanned her face with real concern. "I'll tell you. When I was a boy of eight my mother had an excellent business opportunity in Nice. My family lived up north in Normandy at the time and it was impossible for her to visit frequently. For nearly two years she was mostly away. And yet I remember feeling closer to her in that time than I had before. I wrote long letters and she answered with short ones because her work was taking most of her time. But that did not matter. We formed a deep bond in those letters. I still have them. And I remember being very proud of her for doing what she did."

Jen felt the tears well up in her throat . . . not tears of guilt but tears of gratitude for Robert's generosity and sensitivity. She rolled onto her back and stared up at the sky.

"How beautiful it is here," she sighed. "You know, it's odd. It isn't so unlike Iowa. The air in Duffy is pure and sweet, there's no industry for miles, and although we don't grow grapes, we grow some pretty hefty crops of corn and wheat."

"Hmmm," Robert murmured drowsily, and Jen turned onto her side and squinted at him. He looked at her contentedly through heavily lidded eyes. "The grape has made me groggy." He smiled sleepily.

"Me too." Jen curled up on her side with her arms tucked under her head, feeling pleasantly woozy after two glasses of wine. It seemed perfectly natural to be lying here beside him on the soft plaid blanket he had spread on the ground for their sumptuous repast. How idyllic. How simple and civilized life was here in France.

Drifting, drifting . . . she closed her eyes and felt her body sinking into a deep sleep. Behind her closed lids she saw herself bathed in sunlight, standing alone on the crest of a hill where the grass was high and the wind whipped at her hair as it had earlier in the car. Suddenly she was aware of a tall stalwart figure advancing on her from behind. She smiled, her fingers and breasts tingling with delicious anticipation. Her breathing was quick and shallow as she girded herself for his touch.

In the dream she waited, like a statue, suspended in an agonizing sensual limbo, feeling the warmth of his body as he stood behind her. She arched her neck back slightly in an inviting gesture, and when he stroked her pale white throat with one hand she felt a warm fluidity coursing urgently in her. Eyes closed, she savored the sensation of his expert fingers as they trailed from her ear to her shoulder, exploring the concave spot at the base of her throat and traveling lower until they rested on the plump rise of her breasts.

"Robert . . ." She murmured his name as he grasped her full breasts, pressing his strong vibrating body against her from behind. Without looking she knew that they were his hands. His hands alone could elicit such hot rushing pleasure in her.

He stroked her breasts from behind, inching down into her bra to feel the soft supple flesh. He urged one breast from beneath its confines and probed it gently with his long fingers until she was on fire and whirled around to face him.

"Robert!" she gasped huskily, watching his face, a mask of intent desire.

He did not speak, but his ragged breathing communicated his desire more eloquently than words

51

could ever do. He pulled her down onto the ground and ran his hand over her smooth abdomen. She wriggled closer, hungry to feel his hands on her bare breasts. She was gasping, beside herself with desire, wanting to taste all of him, wanting to know every crevice of his powerfully virile body.

The dream seemed to be sucking her more deeply into its dizzying vortex. Oh, the sensation of his hard, forceful frame pressing against her! She pulled herself closer and felt him do the same, as if they could penetrate the clothing which separated them and prevented them from reveling in that ultimate delicious sensation.

"Jenifer . . . !" His voice seemed to rumble and echo inside her head and for a moment she was reassured that it was still a dream. For a moment she gave in to the delicious sensation of his warm lips pressing against her yielding mouth. Her body began to respond to his insistent demands. It's only a dream, she told herself over and over as he pressed closer, surging with desire. Then suddenly Jen knew what unconsciously she'd been aware of all along—what had been an innocent dream had turned into reality!

She gave an involuntary gasp and tore herself away, a wild-eyed expression on her face. She wasn't dreaming! She bolted to her feet. Her hair was a tumbled mass of red curls, her face was drained. She turned away from his dazed, questioning eyes, her breasts still tingling from his touch.

"It's all right," he soothed in a hushed voice.

She swallowed hard. Of course it was. They had fallen asleep. She had started dreaming. The dream had taken over, invading reality. But only the kiss had been real so it was all right. She shouldn't get upset over a kiss. Everything was fine. There was no reason to be upset.

But she could not move. Her hands were clenched into tight fists, and though she stood motionless she felt herself reeling, turned recklessly upside down.

"Don't be afraid . . ." He reached for her hand and drew her back down onto the ground beside him. "You are very beautiful."

He covered her mouth with a kiss and she lacked the will to fight him. *How could this be happening? How?* As his tongue explored her mouth the same question repeated itself. She wrapped her arms tighter around his neck, answering his torrid kisses with a passion she had never known.

She had to stop!

"Please, don't be afraid," Robert's warm breath titillated her as he spoke. Suddenly she found the resolve to pull her quivering body away from him. Everything was fine. Nothing had really happened. It had only been this kiss. She tugged at the bottom of her sweater as if to reassure herself. It was all so fuzzy, like a fading segment of a dream . . . except for the last few moments.

"Are you all right?" He touched her arm solicitously.

She nodded tightly. "I'll be fine. I guess we must have slept for quite a while." She glanced quickly at the ribbons of pale violet ribbed in pink at the base of the horizon. "I really should be getting on toward Beaune. I want to unpack and get organized before classes start tomorrow."

"Jenifer, I shouldn't like you to be upset . . ."

"I'm not upset with you, Robert," she told him

as she began replacing the little foil parcels from Fauchon in the picnic hamper.

"You're upset with yourself? But why?"

Jenifer felt her temper begin to sizzle. For the first time in her life she felt the urge to throw something. She gripped one of the wine goblets until she felt it begin to give ever so slightly. She tossed it into the hamper with an angry flounce of her tousled red head.

"I'm sorry, Robert. Really . . . I . . ." The day had turned sour. Well, she might have known it would. Last night he had been the one to apologize, today it was her turn. Life, after all, was not a fantasy. She had stupidly allowed herself to be swept away. She told herself she wasn't worried at all about what he thought of her. No, it was how she thought of herself that troubled her. What would have happened if she hadn't waked up? Might she have allowed a man who was almost a total stranger to make love to her? The thought left her shaken.

"Jenifer . . ." Robert knelt down beside her as she busied herself packing up the hamper. He looked earnestly into her face.

"I . . . I just want to go. If you don't mind . . ." Jen looked around with a bewildered expression. "We can talk in the car . . . Look, I am sorry . . ."

"But, dammit, you don't have anything to be sorry for!" Robert took the hamper away from her and headed for the car.

Jen stared after his retreating figure. Why had her apology infuriated him so?

She gathered up the blanket and a few remaining items, including the empty bottle of Burgundy, and ran after him.

54

"Robert . . . ! Really . . . I'm so sorry this happened." There was a familiar note of desperation in her voice as she addressed his broad back.

"There is no need to apologize," he said.

But she could not stop herself. His inexplicable anger triggered some deep response in her and before she could stop herself she had apologized again.

After a moment she climbed dismally into the car, staring blindly out the window as he pulled onto the winding road that would lead them to the highway.

"Look, Jenifer, it's my responsibility as much as yours. Things got a bit out of hand . . . for you. What I mean is . . . you weren't ready. I can understand that. It is your prerogative, after all. I can scarcely blame you for not wanting to kiss a man you've only just met."

She felt a glow shimmer in the pit of her stomach as she realized how fiercely her desire for him had invaded her dreams. It was her fault.

They drove in silence for several long miles, but seeing his unhappiness only intensified her feelings of guilt and remorse. She was the cause of his unhappiness. If only she had behaved more sensibly they wouldn't be riding along like strangers.

"Don't . . ." He gave her a curt look as she opened her mouth to apologize again. "You must not apologize again! Why? Why are you doing that?"

Jenifer felt the tears stinging her eyes. She was suddenly overwhelmed with the years she had spent apologizing. She had spent the last several years of her life apologizing!

"I thought you were angry with me," Jenifer

articulated after a while. "I thought you were mad because I . . . I stopped."

"No." Robert reached over and took her hand firmly. "I was disappointed, not angry. Or if I was angry . . . it was at myself, not at you. How could I be angry at you, Jenifer?"

Jen smiled wanly. "I guess I'm conditioned to think that when anything gets messed up, it's my fault."

"Your husband taught you that?" Robert continued to hold her hand as they drove.

"It sounds like an excuse, doesn't it?"

"Not necessarily. I don't believe you are the sort of woman who makes accusations lightly."

"For a long time," Jen said after a moment, "I didn't realize it was happening. Even when we were in high school Ed had very strong opinions about what I should do, where I should go, what I should wear and who my friends should be. I thought it was because he loved me. When he got mad because I stayed out late with some of my girlfriends, I thought it was because he was so worried about me. I felt terrible to have put him through such anguish. It never occurred to me that eleven o'clock was not all that late and that Duffy, Iowa, is not exactly a crime-ridden city."

Robert nodded understandingly as she continued. "After we were married he became even more . . . protective. That's how I thought of it then. I'd played the organ at our church since I was sixteen, but even before Mike was born Ed would get impatient with me for spending so much time at choir practice. He said he missed me on Wednesday nights and that Sunday was his only real day off, the only day we could be together. Only most Sundays he'd be busy with his friends or

56

else watching some game on television. I'm sorry . . ." Jen caught herself and laughed. "I was going to say I shouldn't be carrying on like this."

"Old habits die hard," Robert observed wryly.

"It was as if everything I did was designed to hurt or belittle him," Jen reflected. "I honestly didn't mean it to."

"Why did you marry him?"

Jen shivered. "I've never told anybody this."

She paused, looking out the window at the rows and rows of grapes that flashed by. "For a very superficial reason—because he was the captain of the football team, because when I was with him it seemed like people envied me."

Robert nodded. Her confession had not shocked him. Jen settled back into her seat with a wistful expression. How easy it was to talk to him, to say things that had remained locked away, some of them even from herself.

"I have a confession to make too." He gave her a mysterious smile. "You and I have something else in common."

Jen studied his handsome profile as he continued. "I married my wife because she was a great beauty, because my friends were impressed that I had won the heart of so fair a maid. I, too, married young. I had scarcely turned twenty. People were always telling us that we made the perfect couple —she so lithe and blond, I so dark . . . how stupid!"

He broke off bitterly and accelerated the car to a crazy speed.

"Robert." Jen touched his arm lightly and he slowed down. But the bitterness remained. The intimacy of the previous moment was shattered by his resentment.

They drove in silence for the next several miles, until Jenifer saw that they had entered the Beaune city limits. She felt a panicky sensation in her stomach at the thought of saying good-bye to him on such a sour note.

"Robert, I understand how painful it can be to separate from someone . . . especially in the beginning."

Robert gave a short cynical laugh. "Oh, I am not lamenting the separation from her. Oh, no! Far from that!"

"Well, I just meant . . ."

"It's not pain I feel . . . believe me!"

His anger intimidated her even though she told herself it was not directed at her. It was as if a door had slammed between them. Robert was somewhere else, locked away with his own memories.

Though it was only five o'clock, it was almost dark when the Citroën entered the small medieval city of Beaune. There was something eerie about the girdle of ramparts surrounding the two-thousand-year-old city. Perhaps it was only that she was both emotionally and physically drained.

"The address of the house where I'll be staying is 8 rue Garat." Jen recited the information.

Robert gave no sign of having heard her, though he appeared to know exactly where he was going. Five minutes later they pulled up in front of a gray stone house with a small iron gate off to the left.

"Number 8," Jen verified as he halted the car.

Robert stared straight ahead with the same remote expression on his face. "Will you mind if I do not help you inside with your luggage?"

"Oh, no!" Jen exclaimed, suddenly eager to extricate herself from the awkward situation. She jumped out of the car, trying not to think, trying not to be disappointed.

Robert opened the car trunk and carried her luggage to the gate. "I'm sure someone will come when you ring."

"Yes, I'm sure they will!" Jen managed a quick smile. "Thank you, Robert."

Robert grasped her hand and held it tightly without looking at her. "Jenifer . . ."

Her heart quickened. He seemed on the point of saying something. . . . Then suddenly he released her hand and hurried back to his car.

CHAPTER FOUR

Madame Pauline bustled Jenifer through the charming courtyard and into the house, an old baronial mansion. Though it had fallen into disrepair, it was nevertheless appealing.

"Everyone else is situated," the elegant white-haired proprietress told her as they climbed a marble staircase to the second floor. The dimly lit hallway was lined with old tapestries and there was a beautiful antique secretary at the far end.

"I didn't think it would be so grand," Jenifer murmured, forgetting about Robert Pierre for a moment as she looked around her room. The orientation letter had described modest living accommodations in a rooming house. She had imagined a rundown clapboard house with a sagging front porch, a musty odor in the parlor and a cramped little bedroom to call her own. Instead she was greeted by a spacious room papered in a delicate rose-patterned design, gleaming oak floors strewn with several well-worn oriental rugs and a rather magnificent four-poster bed covered in a faded pink satin spread.

"It is kind of you to say so." Madame Pauline walked proudly across the room and put another log on the fire that was smoldering in the tiny fireplace. "I lit it mostly for the beautiful effect." She smiled. "And these windows"—Madame opened the heavy shutters with a flourish—"look down on what is left of my garden."

"It's just lovely." Jen ran her hand over the smooth patina of a small writing table.

"We serve *petit déjeuner* from seven until nine and that is the only official meal. Most days the students are too full from the day's tasting, though Monsieur Rennes likes me to keep some soup bubbling and there's always cheese and fruit. There are maps in the parlor and a list of recommended restaurants within walking distance. The others will be gathering in the garden around eight if you want to join them."

"I'm exhausted," Jen told Madame Pauline before the older woman left. "I think it's early to bed for me."

But she could not stop thinking of Robert. What could have happened to make him so bitter? He seemed so incredibly loving, so sensitive and understanding . . . except where his ex-wife was concerned.

"Knock, knock, knock!" Just as Jen finished unpacking and was placing pictures of her sons next to the bed a lilting cheerful voice sang outside her door.

"I'm Nellie Clyde," the portly Englishwoman announced when Jen opened the door. "You and I will have to stick together like-it-or-not because

61

we're the only dames in the class. Mind if I come in?"

Jen stood aside as Nellie bustled past. "Between you and me it's a pretty competitive lot. There's one other American from Chicago, a Mr. Martin, and the rest are all French. I'm English."

"I gathered," Jenifer laughed. "I'm Jenifer Mallory."

"I gathered you were." Nellie laughed and her pink cheeks seemed even plumper. "I'm glad I like you and I'm doubly glad you're an American. No doubt since most of the students are French, the classes will be conducted in french. *Parlez-vous français?*"

"Un peu." Jen felt suddenly nervous. But as Nellie Clyde rattled on about her restaurant outside of Stratford, at least Jen was thinking about something other than Robert Pierre. She found herself laughing at Nellie's descriptions of the other students. Nellie had been in Beaune since the previous day and had already formed very definite opinions about practically everyone, except Monsieur Rennes, whom she had not yet met.

"But I hear he is very handsome." Nellie, who was in her late fifties, plunked down into one of the easy chairs and crossed her legs in readiness for a long gab. "And very temperamental. According to one of the waiters at La Petite Auberge, he literally picked up a man who was assisting in making pastries and tossed him out the kitchen door. Imagine!"

Before Jen could comment, Madame Pauline tapped at the door to tell Jen she had a phone call.

"I'll wait for you," Nellie called after her as she followed Madame Pauline back downstairs to the little phone booth located at the rear of the marble foyer.

Jenifer's heart was in her throat as she reached for the receiver. There couldn't be trouble at home! There just couldn't be! She girded herself.

"Jenifer . . . it's Robert."

"Robert!" Her knees weakened with relief.

"Look, I have to see you. Right away!"

"I can't." She leaned wearily against the closed door. "Robert, I begin classes tomorrow. I'm exhausted."

"You have to have dinner!"

A typically French reply. "No." Jen was resolved. "I'm going straight to bed."

"Jenifer . . ."

"Robert, it's not that I don't want to see you again. I do. But not now. Everything is going too fast. I need time to think. Tomorrow is too important to me. I have to study my French . . . have to get some sleep. You have the address. You could write. Perhaps we could see each other in a few weeks."

"Jenifer . . ."

She opened her mouth to apologize and caught herself. "Please understand," she said, and then she hung up.

"Not bad news, I hope?" Nellie scanned her face anxiously when she returned to her room.

"No, no." Jen collapsed onto her bed, near tears. "Nellie, if you don't mind, I think I'll take a long hot bath and go to bed."

"No dinner? You can't go to bed without dinner!" Nellie exclaimed, and in spite of herself Jen smiled.

According to Meryl Beamen it would take exactly seven days to make the transition from Iowa time to French time, a day for each hour's difference. When Jen awoke the next morning the sky was streaked with gray and it was only five o'clock —almost time for the late-night news in Duffy. Amazingly, though, she felt rested. More important, she felt she had made the right decision in not seeing Robert.

She hummed as she stoked up the remaining coals in the little tiled fireplace. Alone. For the first time in her life she was staking out her own territory. She was not in her parents' house nor under her husband's roof. She turned on a reading light and, still in her robe and slippers, opened her French book to review her verbs. There was absolute stillness in the house and she concentrated with an intensity she had never experienced. When she heard sounds outside in the hallway she looked at her little travel clock. To her surprise it was already seven thirty.

She put her books aside and opened the shutters. Below her was Madame Pauline's garden, a bright profusion of color. She watched as Madame bent to remove some wilted petals on the roses. Then she quickly changed into a pair of jeans and a faded navy-blue University of Iowa sweatshirt. The brochure had said nothing about class attire, no obligatory chef's white. And this was her favorite cooking outfit. So what if she didn't look stylish. She was here to learn to cook!

She pulled her hair back into a smooth ponytail, put on white socks and tennis shoes and looked at herself in the oval mirror. The contrast between the faded elegance of her room and her very midwestern collegiate attire made her smile. She felt good. More like herself than she had yesterday in Paris, more like herself than she had in years!

Downstairs in Madame's kitchen she was greeted by Nellie and Eric Martin, the only other American in the group.

"We've met before." The handsome blond man rose. He gave Jenifer a pointed smile which implied a familiarity she was not certain she appreciated. He paused dramatically, as if he expected her to rush into his arms.

"Give the girl a chance to have a bit of coffee," Nellie joshed.

Jen poured a cup full of the thick aromatic coffee and racked her brain to think of where she might have met such a citified, sophisticated man. Certainly not in Duffy. And most of her acquaintances during her short stay in Des Moines had worked at Ed's factory. She returned to sit beside Nellie at the old pine table. She met Eric Martin's smiling blue eyes evenly. "I'm afraid you have me there, Mr. Martin."

He laughed as if the two of them were in league. "Three guesses."

Beneath the table, Nellie nudged Jen's leg with her knee, clearly communicating her disdain for his egocentric behavior. As if anyone could forget meeting Eric Martin!

Jen sipped her coffee, her face drawn in deep concentration. After several moments and only out of sheer desperation, she said, "Chicago."

"Of course!" He smiled and folded his arms across the front of his tight-fitting white T-shirt, which stated, "I'm okay."

Chicago? She had met him in Chicago?

"Try some of Madame's raspberry preserves."

Nellie thrust a blue crock at Jenifer to cover the awkward pause.

Eric's blue eyes sparkled flirtatiously. She had drawn a total blank. The contest? He must have had something to do with the contest. She darted him a quick look. He had a suave, affluent look, so it was doubtful if he had been another contestant. Also, 97 percent of the contestants had been women, so that line of thinking was probably wrong.

"I don't know." Jen was not adept at game playing.

"Oh, come on." Eric kicked her tennis shoe lightly under the table and something in her bristled.

Suddenly it came to her! The supercilious judge who had looked more like a tennis pro than the owner of one of Chicago's hottest new restaurants.

"I'm responsible for your being here." He grinned modestly, as if to finally set the record straight.

"Did you whisper her prize-winning recipe into her ear?" Nellie asked with a wry smile. "And did you bake it as well?"

While Jen and Nellie munched away on the crusty bread slathered with sweet butter and topped with Madame's delicious preserves, Eric Martin enlightened them as to his own culinary success. His was the only restaurant in Chicago to have been admitted to the famed Michelin Guide in the past ten years. His was the only restaurant in Chicago where one had to phone for reservations a month in advance. His *potage crème de cresson* had been heralded by Mimi Sheraton.

"Then I must have misunderstood," said Nellie at the conclusion of his tireless monologue. "I thought you said you were here to *study* with Monsieur Rennes."

Jenifer removed their dishes to the sink in order to hide her approving smile.

But Nellie's none too subtle dig escaped him nonetheless. He had rented a car for the six-week period and wanted to give Jen and Nellie a lift to the Petite Auberge, which was located in the countryside south of Beaune.

"We've got our bikes, haven't we, ducks?" Nellie jumped in quickly, thus rescuing Jen from the unpleasant prospect of a ride with the self-aggrandizing Chef Martin.

"It's nearly four miles." Eric threw his fashionable leather jacket over one shoulder.

"Good for what ails you." Nellie patted her ample hips.

"Yes," Jen chimed in. "I need all the exercise I can get!"

"Did you ever?" Nellie asked as she accompanied Jen to a nearby bike shop so that Jen could rent a bike. "Perhaps he is a brilliant chef. He certainly has the ego for it."

"It should be interesting." Jen grinned. "This all seems terribly important to him."

"Well, it's terribly important to me," Nellie admitted as they pedaled along a tree-lined country road some time later. "I've been languishing in my little tea shop for fifteen years. Finally managed to scrape together enough pounds to fix up the derelict kitchen and spruce the place up. Nothing impresses the British like a certificate from a bona fide three-star French chef. Who knows, I may even call the place Madame Nellie's."

Jen laughed. It felt good to get some exercise, and in Nellie's company she felt her own optimism begin to blossom. Even though Nellie already had her own business there was a lot at stake for her too. Yes, there was far too much at stake to risk an emotional involvement. She couldn't let herself be distracted by a handsome Frenchman. Even if Robert did try to get in touch with her again, she would not respond.

Up ahead, rising out of the gently rolling fields like a delicately etched painting in a child's book of fairy tales, was La Petite Auberge. The spectacular stone castle, replete with crenellated towers and turrets, dated back to 1447, when the last Duke of Burgundy died and Beaune was finally annexed to the crown of France.

"La Petite Auberge?" Jen looked inquiringly at Nellie. Why on earth had Monsieur Rennes named his establishment "Little House"?

"You've got me, ducks," Nellie puffed as they turned off the main road and coasted down a little hill before making the final ascent to the Auberge. "Unless Monsieur Rennes has a very wry sense of humor. Maybe it's a bit like me renaming my restaurant Madame Nellie's Bistro!"

"Maybe you're right," Jen called as she pedaled past Nellie on her way to the top of the hill.

"Don't wait for me," Nellie gasped after her.

By the time Jen reached the top her face was flushed and she felt a dampness along her spine. She turned to see Nellie walking her bike up the hill. But the ride had further fortified her. Good heavens, she hadn't ridden a bike since high school, though her two older boys both had bikes. Back in Duffy it never occurred to her to go riding along the beautiful country roads, which were lined on either side with high corn in the summer. Oh, she would return to Duffy so svelte and shapely that everyone would gasp at the change in her. Meryl Beamen, who had warned her again and again about gaining weight because of all the delicious bread and yummy pastries, would, for once, be rendered speechless!

She drank in the cool fresh autumn air and admired the beautifully manicured formal gardens that surrounded the castle. Maybe Nellie was wrong about the name being merely a joke. Although it was true that the castle was enormous, there was a delicacy in its design, something magical about its graceful parapets and slender towers. La Petite Auberge! Yes, she understood completely why Monsieur Rennes had named it that.

"Here we are, Jenifer . . . over here!" Nellie had passed her and was steering her bike toward a small stone building beyond a grove of tall pine trees.

"The teaching kitchen is separate from the restaurant kitchen," Nellie explained as she leaned her bike against a tree.

"Come." Nellie took Jen's hand and led her through a heavy wooden door into the most enormous and beautiful kitchen she had ever seen.

"Incroyable, non?" A small wiry Frenchman smiled at Jen.

"Not bad, eh?" Nellie grinned.

"Not bad at all." Jen nodded at Eric Martin, who, along with the rest of the class, was seated around the outside perimeter of a large marble counter. Above the counter was a large skylight through which the morning sun spilled in onto a variety of flowering plants that were scattered over the terra-cotta tiled floor.

"Come." Nellie beckoned to Jen and she followed her around to the inside of the L-shaped counter, which was lined with wide, open shelves. Every known cooking accouterment was in evidence, everything from the ubiquitous food processors to heavy-duty machines for kneading bread, to ten-speed mixers, flan circles, molds of every shape and size and the most enormous wire whisks she had ever seen. On the open end of the counter were two gleaming restaurant ranges with an impressive collection of overhanging copper pots and pans. There were two large refrigerators separated by a span of two-foot-thick butcher block whose surface clearly reflected years of chopping and slicing with the impressive set of knives which hung on the wall above. Everything was spotless, gleaming in the morning sun.

"So what do you think?" The small wiry Frenchman who had caught Jen's eye sauntered over.

The teaching kitchen was beautiful, elegant and somehow terrifying in its professionalism. Jen concentrated on replying to the Frenchman in his native tongue. *"Je ne sais pas* (I don't know)," she replied honestly. "It is beautiful!"

Something in her tightened as she met his sardonic eyes. So this was the famous Pierre Rennes and she was somehow already off on the wrong foot.

"You are the American, I take it." He fixed her with his small dark eyes just as Nellie intervened.

"Jenifer, this is Albert Jamin."

Jen thrust her hand forward, relieved that the small man who had taken an obvious dislike to her was not the famous chef. As Nellie, the self-appointed hostess cum translator, went down the line introducing the other men, Jen smiled and shook hands, feeling oddly as if she were on display. Nellie's French was far superior to hers.

Even Eric Martin had a consummate grasp of the language as he conversed in his animated manner with Edgard Moreau, a dapper gray-haired man who was the oldest student in the class. How in the world was she going to survive with her elementary French?

"Où est Monsieur Rennes?" she articulated after all of the introductions were complete.

"Always late," Albert Jamin replied in halting English. "It is part of his charm . . . part of his aura."

There was an air of tension and excitement as they sat at the marble counter exchanging stories about the temperamental chef.

"I hear he is in danger of losing his third star," Maurice Goulart, a slender young man from Normandy, remarked in a light voice.

"Oh, no!" Edgard protested vehemently. "That will never happen. It is only a rumor. People like to talk because of the divorce. I'm sure of it."

Edgard turned to Jen with a quiet dignified smile and explained in English. "Monsieur Rennes has been much in the headlines lately . . . though I don't imagine his divorce is exactly international news. But the French love nothing more than to dwell on any possible heartbreak or scandal where love or the loss of same is concerned. Monsieur Rennes was married to Catherine Rennes."

"The movie star?" Jen felt herself being drawn into the gossipy atmosphere.

Edgard nodded. *"Oui,* Catherine Rennes. The one and only Catherine."

"The one and only Catherine," Albert repeated with a lustful smile that reduced a few of the other men, including Eric Martin, to laughter.

71

Of course everyone knew Catherine Rennes, but somehow Jen had not connected her with Pierre Rennes. Catherine Rennes had burst into stardom when she was only eighteen years old, appearing as a seductively beautiful rich nymphette in the classic Porret film about the French aristocracy. Although it was not the sort of film to have made it to Duffy, Jen had read about its explicitly erotic scenes and in later years had seen the ravishing Catherine in several Hollywood films.

"It's a pity really," Edgard went on, "that such rumors begin. I'm sure Monsieur Rennes has enough on his hands with all of his legal entanglements without having to combat rumors about his dwindling culinary standards. Judging from the dinner I had at the Auberge last month, he is in no danger of losing anything."

"You ate there?" Jen gasped. Reputedly a meal for one at the Petite Auberge ran anywhere from eighty dollars to well over a hundred. Edgard was obviously no starving cooking student.

"It was a splurge, dear girl," the older man laughed gently. "Lest any of you cast me in the role of the eccentric dilettante, let me assure you it was a rare occasion. The pension of a retired schoolteacher does not afford me such luxuries as a matter of course."

"A schoolteacher?" Nellie cried delightedly. "You're a schoolteacher, are you?"

"A retired math teacher who always wanted to be a chef," Edgard chuckled.

"That's wonderful," Jen enthused.

"Yes. I don't yet own my own restaurant but I'm looking for a spot in the South, somewhere in Provence."

72

"Gook luck." Jen clasped Edgard's hand. As far as she could determine they were the only two who did not already own their own restaurants.

"Well, from what I hear"—Albert Jamin returned from gazing out the window—"Monsieur Rennes was the one to leave Catherine. Madame Pauline told my cousin that it is common knowledge here in Beaune that he has for years been having an affair with the woman he calls his assistant. I believe her name is Jeannete DuBois."

"Oh!" Nellie chimed in, "I met her. Oh, she's beautiful!"

Jen felt as though her neck was on a swivel as she turned from Nellie to Albert, to Edgard to Jean to Maurice, all of whom had some tasty morsel to contribute. She smiled thinking how Meryl Beamen would have felt right at home in the midst of such a juicy bilingual gossip fest.

After another hour had passed, the atmosphere, which had been tense and suspenseful, was tinged with hostility.

"Who the hell does he think he is?" Eric Martin paced irritably to the door. Jenifer had to agree with him.

Just then the door flew open and everyone tensed. But instead of Chef Rennes they were greeted by a chic, elegantly dressed woman who introduced herself as Jeannete DuBois, Monsieur Rennes's assistant.

"Monsieur wishes me to apologize to you most heartily." She caught Jenifer's eye and spoke in a halting tone, enunciating each syllable clearly.

She looked just like the ladies in Paris, Jen thought, admiring Mademoiselle DuBois' sleek short blond hair, the trim cut of her red knit sweater and slim red skirt, which she wore with black stockings and black high heels.

"Unfortunately this morning's session will be canceled but Monsieur Rennes has asked me to assure you that the class will be made up at a later time. He expects to have completed his business in plenty of time for the afternoon session. In the meantime please feel free to familiarize yourselves with the teaching kitchen."

Jeannete gave an ingratiating smile as she crossed back to the open door. "Welcome to La Petite Auberge."

For a moment no one spoke. Jeannete DuBois' appearance had acted as a tonic to soothe the irritable mood of the class. Monsieur Rennes's beautiful emissary had done her job.

As Nellie and Jen were climbing back onto their bikes Albert intercepted Jenifer. *"Pardon moi*, madame, but if I could be of service to you . . . I mean, in helping you with your French."

"Oh . . . thank you." Jen forced herself to smile. There was an obsequiousness in his manner that made her nervous. She had noticed him watching the others earlier as if to glean information on their reactions which would later prove valuable. She had not reckoned on such a competitive group. And Albert, on the surface at least, seemed the most competitive of the lot.

"Perhaps this evening," he offered, hooking his thumbs into his belt.

"I think I need a few more days to settle in," Jen said pleasantly. "Maybe later when I've recovered from my jet lag." Since she had felt his immediate disdain upon meeting him, why on earth would he want to give her French lessons?

God bless jet lag, she thought as she parked her

74

bike in the little shed outside the kitchen door at Madame Pauline's. Jet lag provided her with innumerable convenient excuses. With a stab, she thought of Robert.

She shook her head abruptly and went up to her room and changed into a pair of tan slacks and a white turtleneck sweater, which she wore with a brown-and-beige checked blazer. Since the afternoon session was not until three she decided to take a walk around the town.

She walked to the center of the village admiring the perfectly preserved fifteenth-century hospice, which was one of the world's richest and most renowned hospitals. The hospice owned some of the most illustrious vineyards in the region. She wasn't meeting Nellie for lunch until noon so she entered the Gothic masterpiece and spent the next hour looking at Flemish-Burgundian art in the museum wing of the hospital. There was so much to do in the region. Already she felt drawn to the history of the Dukes of Burgundy. It was all so accessible, too, as if past and present and future were all inexorably interwoven into a fine tapestry.

The minute she stepped back outside into the midday sun her eye was drawn to a yellow Citroën parked at an odd angle in front of one of the large wine stores. Her heart leaped inside her breast but she forced herself to turn the other way, telling herself that there was more than one yellow Citroën in all of France.

Damn! She stopped walking suddenly. What if the car was Robert's? What if he had come back?

Romantic drivel. She chastised herself and headed for the bistro where she was meeting Nellie. But she was early and, once inside, unable to contain her curiosity, she phoned Madame Pauline's to see if anyone had left a message for her. Of course the answer was no, and for her trouble she was left with a dull ache in her heart. She took a seat at a small table with a red-and-white-checked cloth and waited for Nellie.

Lunch left her feeling even more alone, for Nellie was unable to contain her excitement about Edgard Moreau.

"Ducks, forgive me," Nellie said as they parted company in front of Madame Pauline's after a quick meal. "You don't know what a dearth of decent, kind, attractive men there are when you're my age. Between you and me, I'd given up thinking this old heart would ever accelerate past a modest little trot. This morning it was positively galloping. Not that I came here looking for a man, mark you. Heavens, no! Last thing I had in mind. And a Frenchman at that. But he's asked to drive me to the Auberge and . . ."

"I understand." Jen patted her arm fondly.

"I'll see you out there." She waved as Nellie climbed into Edgard's rusty blue Renault.

"You're welcome to hitch a ride," he called.

"No, I prefer to bike out."

"Good!" Albert Jamin's voice startled her. She turned to find him straddling a bike himself. She knew he had a car, so obviously he had just rented a bike.

Several of the other male students came out of Madame Pauline's and threw her and Albert a curious glance as they pedaled off. Good heavens, the atmosphere was like that of a spy novel, everyone casting furtive glances at everyone else. Was there really that much at stake for all of them?

Fortunately class was starting soon so they

didn't have time for a leisurely ride and conversation. From time to time she glanced at the wiry man beside her. It was odd that he'd wanted to ride with her. Well, maybe she had misjudged him. Maybe he didn't dislike her after all.

By the time they reached the final incline Jen lacked the stamina to make it up the hill so she climbed off her bike and walked.

Albert, who had paced himself, passed her. "It's almost three," he called over his shoulder.

Jen gasped for air. Her side ached from the exertion and her cheeks were bright with color. She paused midway to catch her breath and wipe her brow. Reaching the top of the hill, she was nearly overcome by waves of dizziness.

Then she saw a yellow Citroën parked in the center of the driveway.

She stared at the car, thunderstruck, unable or unwilling to acknowledge what possible meaning it might have.

"Hurry!" Albert tugged at her arm. "If you do not want to be off on the . . . how do you say . . . wrong foot . . ."

But Jenifer was too dazed to respond, for at that very minute Robert emerged from inside the Petite Auberge and jumped into his car.

"Robert!" she called without thinking, knowing only that the sight of him had banished her resolution to forget him.

"Robert!" She waved as he backed the Citroën into a parking space, jumped out and hurried around to the rear of the Auberge. Jen glanced quickly at Albert, who was regarding her with a quizzical smile. Obviously Robert had come out to find her.

77

"Robert!" Finally he heard her and turned around.

"I have class," she called to him across one of the gardens. "I'm finished at five-thirty if you want to meet me. I can't talk now!"

"Jenifer! Wait!" He started toward her.

But she couldn't afford to be late. She would have to trust that he would meet her later. She dashed around the stone building and dropped her bike onto the ground.

"You're sure you don't want to talk to your lover?" Albert smiled insinuatingly.

"What do you mean . . . my lover?" Jen was fed up with all the intrigue. This was a cooking school, not an espionage institute. She ran toward the door.

"No wonder you weren't worried about being tardy." Albert cut in front of her with his hand on the doorknob.

"What are you talking about?" Jen's dark eyes blazed.

He turned to her and said, sotto voce, "Competing against Pierre Rennes's new lover is hardly fair play," he murmured.

And then it dawned on her. As Jen followed him into the classroom, the faces seated around the marble countertop were a blur. She climbed onto one of the high stools and clasped her hands tightly in an effort to control herself.

Robert Pierre was Pierre Rennes.

She heard the door open, felt a draft, heard his footsteps as he crossed to the center of the room behind the marble counter. The intensity of her fury had turned her heart to stone. She felt his dark eyes on her but did not look.

"Bonjour." His low voice was unusually husky. "I am Pierre Rennes and I am looking forward to spending the next six weeks with all of you."

CHAPTER FIVE

For the next two hours Jenifer felt as if she were a zombie, an emotionless automaton going through a ritual. She could not afford to think, could not risk considering why he had carried on such a charade.

They were working on *pâte à chou* (puff pastry), and for two grueling hours she averted her eyes from his face. She watched his large sensitive hands measure the floor, then beat it into the heated water and milk mixture.

"It is very important not to work the dough too long," he said, "or the puffs will not rise correctly."

He repeated everything in English. She knew it was for her benefit.

She hardened herself as he beat the dough vigorously and began adding the beaten eggs. When it came time to repeat the process herself, she positioned herself between Nellie and Edgard and moved away on some pretext whenever he approached. He did not address her by her name as he did the other students. He observed her tech-

80

nique with the dough and made several suggestions in a strictly professional tone.

It was inevitable that they would touch, arms brushing arms as he reached across one of the baking sheets to dust a long éclair with confectioner's sugar.

"It will hold its shape better during baking," he announced to the rest of the class as he stood behind Jenifer indicating the single éclair. "And they should be baked as quickly as possible."

It was torture to be in the same room with him. At times she felt her throat constrict. No, she would not think. Not now. She struggled for composure.

Everyone in the class was working to please him. Everyone wanted to be best, to excel, to be singled out. It would have been a tense situation even if they hadn't met before. Now it was impossible.

But only Albert knew that she knew him. Maybe she could tell Albert she had mistaken him for someone else. After all, she had called him Robert. Yes, if she could keep the whole thing secret, she might salvage the situation for herself. It would still be difficult, but at least she wouldn't have to contend with the resentment of the rest of the class.

Pierre Rennes's low laughter interrupted her train of thought. He was standing next to Nellie, who was having a difficult time getting her dough the proper consistency to come out of the pastry bag.

"I'm all thumbs when it comes to pastry." Nellie was totally exasperated.

"You have to get the *feel* of it." Pierre smiled

patiently and Jen turned away in a panic. How could she endure the next six weeks?

She walked over to the oven and removed her sheet of éclairs and ovals, amazed that they had held their shape perfectly and browned to a delicate color without one single puff cracking open.

"Very nice . . ." Pierre's warm breath grazed the back of her neck and she shivered. Everything inside tightened as she watched him cross to help Edgard and Maurice fill their large Paris-Brests with an almond pastry cream that had been prepared earlier by a member of Pierre's cooking staff.

She glanced at the clock. It was past five-thirty. Thank God! She removed the cooled puffs from her baking sheet and slipped them gingerly into the plastic bags as she had been told to do. She put them in the freezer, whisked her dishes into the dishwasher and fled out the back door.

What could she think? What could she possibly think of a man who lied about who he was? She pedaled furiously to Madame Pauline's, ran upstairs and locked the door to her room as if she could lock out all of her bewildered feelings. He had toyed with her. Her cheeks burned thinking of it.

"Jenifer!" Madame Pauline was tapping at her door. "You have a phone call."

"I'm busy." Jen stiffened. Of course he would be calling. He would have to say something.

"It's Mademoiselle DuBois from the Auberge, dear. She says it's rather important."

Jen jumped to her feet and went downstairs. So he got his mistress to make his apology phone calls, did he? She was shaking when she picked up the receiver.

82

"You must let me explain!" a deep voice demanded. It was not Mademoiselle DuBois after all!

"There is nothing to say," Jen said numbly.

"Oh, yes, there is. I owe you one hell of an explanation and you're going to get it tonight . . . over dinner."

She closed her eyes, feeling trapped.

"I wanted to tell you who I was," he went on urgently. "That's why I called last night after I dropped you off."

"Rob . . ." Jen broke off. She was near tears and all she wanted to do was slam the phone down.

"Jenifer . . . ? I'm coming by for you at ten. I'm sorry it can't be earlier but I have a show to run out here. Please . . . take a nap and try not to condemn me until you hear what I have to say."

Upstairs, Jen threw herself on her bed and stared miserably out the window into the dusk. What could he possibly say to change the hopeless feeling that had come over her? No! She would not be here when he came.

She rolled over onto her stomach and buried her head in her arms. He had humiliated her by lying, by listening to her prattle on about Duffy and her naive dream of opening her own restaurant. My God, she had actually explained cooking terms to him, thinking that he, like most men, knew little about such things.

She sprang to her feet with a vengeful, angry look on her face. If only she could hurt him in some way.

Suddenly she was sobbing uncontrollably. She stripped off her clothes and went into the tiny bathroom and stood under a warm shower. What was happening to her? She had been through ten years of marriage and a divorce and never felt so

83

much anger and resentment for another person. Robert . . . Pierre . . . seemed to bring out the worst in her.

She turned her face up to the coursing water and cried harder, cried as if her heart would break.

She emerged from the shower in a more subdued state and stared at her reflection in the mirror. Who was she? For the second time in the past few days the question posed itself.

In the past the answer had been easy. She was Fred and Margaret Ryan's daughter, Teddy and Annie's sister, Ed's wife, Mike, Timmy and David's mother. She was the church organist, assistant den mother, a good cook. Only now none of those labels seemed adequate.

Who was she?

The violent passions which stirred in her breast terrified her. And how was it possible that in the midst of her humiliation and fury there was a relentless desire tugging deep inside her? She wanted him, even now. A warm, surging sensation licked and taunted her. *Wanted him* . . . the words were so foreign they had the ring of another language. And yet she was furious with him. But it would be stupid to allow her wounded pride to dictate her behavior. He was her teacher. First and foremost, he was her teacher and she was here to learn. He was the one who would issue the certificate that would open the doors to her culinary future. Like it or not, she needed him.

Never in her life had she been faced with such a complex, demanding situation. But she was determined. And the first order of business was to phone him and say that she would meet him at a restaurant rather than have someone see him picking her up here. Those were her terms, and all things considered they were more than fair.

She dressed casually in the slacks she had worn earlier and a blue silk blouse. Then she went downstairs to phone the Auberge. She left a message with Jeannete DuBois that she would meet Monsieur Rennes at Maxine's, where she and Nellie had lunched earlier that day.

What must Jeannete DuBois think? Forget about her, she told herself as she walked down the deserted street. Nellie and Edgard Moreau were lingering in Madame Pauline's rose garden, and she fought back feelings of envy, hearing them laughing, seeing the ease and simplicity of their budding romance.

She walked briskly, fairly certain that it was late enough not to encounter any of the other students, particularly Albert. Still she felt nervous, as if she were doing something terribly illicit in meeting Pierre Rennes.

Inside the cozy little bistro she ordered a glass of wine. Her pulse accelerated every time the door opened. And even though she told herself this was the last time they would be meeting this way, she could not still her racing heart or dull the bright, expectant look on her face.

The moment he came through the door she knew it was going to be even more difficult than she had anticipated. He shrugged off his trench coat and sat down across from her, grasping her hands, piercing her with his dark urgent eyes.

"Jenifer, please let me explain," he began before she could cut him off. "When I first saw you at the Deux Magots in Paris I swear to you I had no idea you were on your way to La Petite Auberge as one of my students! I saw only a beautiful young

85

American, someone who was not tired, someone who was radiant and happy. You exuded such joy I could not take my eyes off of you. It had been years since I had looked at a woman as I looked at you. It is not my usual pastime, regardless of what you may think now."

Jenifer stared miserably at her hands, which were locked in his.

"When I saw that you were having difficulty I decided it was fate. Not that I believe in fate, but that is the word I used to give myself permission to spring to your rescue. Normally I am not a forward person, but I could not help myself. If you recall, one of my first questions to you was what had brought you to France. So even before we introduced ourselves . . . I knew . . . I was stunned at the coincidence but by then I knew something about you. I knew that in many ways you were uncertain, diffident. I guessed that if you knew I was the man you would be studying with, you would not feel so comfortable with me."

He paused as if he were waiting for her confirmation. She nodded slightly. He was right. She would not have felt at ease with him had she known he was to be her teacher, the famous Pierre Rennes.

"I felt very close to you," Pierre said softly. "I liked you and felt you liked me. It was so easy to be with you. So simple. I wanted to keep it that way for as long as possible . . . if only for that day."

He released her hands and reached into his jacket pocket and removed his leather wallet. He sorted through a few cards and handed her one of his plastic credit cards.

"When I dine out—in Paris but also sometimes in the provinces—I use the name of Robert Pierre so that I will not be recognized. Most people do not know me by sight . . . only by name. It's easier for everyone. So . . . I decided to be Robert Pierre with you. I was happy to put aside Pierre Rennes, to be simply a man who was falling in love with a woman."

"Don't say that." Jen felt a lump rise in her throat.

"I have to say what is true. You can't deny it. It was beginning to happen. Neither of us wanted it to happen. You and I are both traditionalists . . . we like to think that events occur in a logical, time-ordered way. Even falling in love. But there was something very special happening between us from the very first moment."

Jenifer met his eyes reluctantly as he exerted a warm, intimate pressure on her hands.

"Or maybe we did want it to happen." He leaned across the table until their lips were almost touching. "Maybe in some deep secret spot within ourselves we wanted . . ."

"Robert . . ." Jen pulled her hands away. "Pierre . . ."

In spite of his earnestness, he smiled. "I know. It is frightfully confusing."

"It's *too* confusing!" Jen wished she could feel even a shred of the anger and resentment she had felt earlier. But he was so truly sorry, so intent on making her understand why he had lied, that she was even more attracted to him than before. She thought of all the gossip about him, all the stories of his egotistical, tyrannical nature. Then she thought of how patient he had been with Nellie, how sensitive and accurate he had been in judging her. He was absolutely right. Had he introduced himself as Pierre Rennes she would have closed up tighter than a clam.

"I must say"—his face relaxed into a genuine smile—"I was very impressed with the way you handled yourself in class today."

"I was mortified." Jen found herself actually laughing.

"You seemed in complete control." He chuckled. Pierre signaled the waiter and ordered a cognac for himself and another glass of wine for Jenifer.

"What will you have for dinner?" His eyes caressed her face tenderly.

"I'm really not hungry," Jen said. "And . . . and don't say I have to eat!"

Pierre nodded, then turned serious again. "You do believe me? How sorry I am for all of this confusion between us? Once I'd started the lie I wasn't altogether certain how to get out of it. I kept hoping I could think of the perfect way to explain. I knew it had to be before the first class. That's why I canceled the morning class."

"You're kidding!" Jen exclaimed.

"Don't you see"—he leaned forward again—"how important this was to me. I am not a man who enjoys playing games."

"I know that." Jenifer allowed herself to be drawn into the thrilling power of his dark gaze. The air between them swelled with a highly charged sensuality. She felt her mind quivering on the brink of some exalted abyss. How she wanted to taste him, to savor, if only for a moment, the excruciating pleasure of his touch.

Why did it seem as if she had known him forever? How was it possible to feel so much in so short a time?

As if he had read her mind he said, "It's strange, isn't it? We both married at a young age people we had known—or thought we had known—all of our lives. And now, through some bizarre twist of fate, we meet, and after only . . ."

He broke off as if he knew there was no need for him to complete the sentence. They stared at each other. Her breath grew short and shallow and she had the sense that even though they were not touching they were breathing in unison. She felt her breasts swell and her nipples harden as if they were already pressed against his chest. She longed to stroke his warm flesh, to feel him close against her.

"Come home with me," he whispered. "Let me make love to you."

How was it possible that he could arouse her to such a peak with only his eyes, with his words, with the tantalizing prospect of what it would be like? She shook her head, but he didn't seem to notice her weak protest.

In a daze, she watched him pay the bill and joke casually with the older woman who owned the Bistro. Wasn't he worried that their innocent meeting would be all over town tomorrow? What about Jeannete DuBois? What about Catherine Rennes? What about her own future?

Outside in the autumn air she balked as he steered her to his car, which was parked around the corner in a narrow cobblestone alley.

"Rob . . . Pierre . . . I can't go home with you!"

"It's not too soon, *ma chère*, I swear to you. In your heart you know that time is irrelevant. I know that you understand that as well as I do!"

Suddenly she was in his arms and the passion

that had grown during the sizzling silence and the looks passing between them burst out in full force. Pierre pulled her tightly to him until she was inflamed by the hot, hard intensity of his desire. His tongue foraged deep inside her mouth, promising her an erotic fulfillment of which she had never even dreamed.

His slow exploration of her awakened her to a boldness she had never experienced and she answered his hard kisses with quick fiery kisses of her own. Her lips clung to his, and when he pulled away to open the car door she drew his mouth back, nipping lightly at his lips.

Her mind and her body seemed on the point of exploding as he pulled her inside the car and shut the door. He swiveled her around on the seat until they were pressed, torso to torso, kissing, caressing, tasting each other with a delirious frenzy. Jen ran her hands through his thick coarse hair as he pressed his hands against the small of her back, tilting her hips forward. In one movement he lifted her and turned her until she was facing him, sitting astride his lap, feeling the throbbing in herself as she pressed against him. She sank against him, lost in the hot sensual stirring. He thrust softly up against her and the heat seemed to penetrate through her clothing. Her entire body felt ravaged to the point of some illuminating agony which could be alleviated only by Pierre Rennes.

She needed to be held in his arms, to be locked within them. She needed to feel him inside her!

Oh, it would be all right. There would be only tonight. She had to have him, had to fill the void and stop the ache.

"You have been waiting for me," he murmured

as his hand slipped inside her blouse beneath her bra and found her breast.

It was true! How had she existed without his touch? She arched into him, moaning as he teased her nipple, feeling the sensation turn her very core hard. Jenifer wriggled against him as his tongue moved in and out of her mouth, bringing her closer and closer to that wondrous oblivion. They could not draw apart.

"I will make you so happy." He withdrew his hand from her tingling breast. Panting heavily, he unzipped her slacks and ran his hand inside against her warm, smooth abdomen. "I will make you sing, *ma chère.*" His hand was lightning, trailing currents of stinging fire lower and lower until she shifted and he skimmed beneath her panties. She threw her head back, gasping at the touch of his fingers. Her mind was a blur. Instinctively she turned to give him more freedom of movement. She was wild now and the connection between them was a raging unquenchable fire.

She cried out, once, twice. He had set her off into another realm of desire and she was climbing higher and higher with each sensation.

"I knew you would be beautiful." He covered her mouth with a searing kiss. "This is just the beginning, *ma chère.* For us . . . this is only a beginning! I am like new with you." He withdrew his hand and rested it on her shoulder as he gazed at her.

Jenifer swallowed hard, trying to orient herself. He ran both of his hands gently over her breasts. His lips were parted and his breathing was still ragged with desire. Her breasts ached for more.

"Do you understand what I am saying?" he asked passionately.

91

Jenifer nodded mutely. She understood perfectly.

"I am thirty-five years old," he said. "Not that old. Not old at all. But I had begun to feel so weary . . . not of my work. That was the one area in which I still felt some excitement. But it is not enough, is it? It is not enough to wake up in the morning and feel tired, to wonder where the days went when at one time each dawn broke like a great promise."

Jenifer drew in a steadying breath and took his hand in hers and kissed it. She felt sick with the knowledge that she was going to disappoint him, that this happiness could not last. Her shoulders tensed in readiness. If only they could have been magically transported to his house. If only he had been able to keep touching her, keep kissing her so that her mind could have remained mercifully still. If only reason had not intervened. She shook herself, zipped up her slacks and straightened her blouse and her hair. In the stillness she knew that he had already read her mind, had already sensed her hesitation.

"I am not always a realistic person," he said, opening the car door and standing for a moment before walking around to the driver's side of the car.

He climbed inside and sat slumped behind the wheel. "You are right, of course," he said finally. "It would be indelicate to . . ." He turned to her with an ironic smile. "I don't suppose you would believe that I have a rule about never becoming romantically involved with any of my students, with anyone on my staff for that matter?"

Jen sighed. "I believe you," she said, thinking of all the rumors about Pierre and Jeannete DuBois.

"I want to make an exception with you." He tried for a light bantering tone and shrugged as he realized he had failed.

"Don't worry"—he gave her a beseeching look —"no one saw us. Madame Foucart, who owns the Bistro, is one of the few discreet ladies in Beaune. I doubt she was playing the voyeur when we were inside, and no one wanders into this little alleyway at this hour. It's a freight entrance, reserved for trucks transporting wine."

Jen nodded dismally. She hadn't even been worried about that. For those brief minutes she had totally lost touch with reality.

"What are we going to do?" Pierre looked even larger hunched over the steering wheel.

"Nothing," Jen said after several moments.

"What do you mean?"

She looked at him briefly. He knew precisely what she meant.

"I mean we're not going to do anything." Her voice was barely a whisper. "We're not going to see each other . . . like this anymore."

"It could be arranged, Jenifer," he said with a note of urgency in his voice. "Beaune is a small town, word does travel fast, but it could be arranged."

Jenifer stiffened. Was he so certain it could be arranged because he had arranged such secretive little rendezvous before? Was that what had driven Catherine Rennes out of his life?

"We could meet in Dijon." He took her arm and turned her to face him. But he saw the look in her eye and he released her with a hopeless shrug.

"We are going to do nothing," Jen repeated flatly. "We are not going to see each other outside class. You are not going to give me preferential treatment nor, I hope, make things difficult for me."

"I know how important all this is to you." He turned her to face him again.

"I hope you do." Jen met his eyes evenly. "I don't want any favors from you."

"It will be hard not to grant you . . ."

"But you mustn't give me any special consideration!" Jen cried.

"It happens that you are one of the best . . ."

"No," Jen interrupted. "I was watching the others today, too. I have a lot to learn. Maurice's technique far surpasses mine, so does Edgard's and . . . Albert Jamin's."

"You are not a good judge of yourself, Jenifer." Pierre smiled softly, then leaned forward to kiss her gently. "Please, don't decide anything tonight. Say that you will meet me on Sunday evening. I will make a reservation at a little guesthouse I know in Dijon. No one will suspect a thing. You can say you are going to look at the cathedral, there is much to see there. It will all seem perfectly plausible."

"Rob . . . Pierre . . . damn!" Jenifer slammed her hand against the dashboard in an uncharacteristic display of temperament.

"Call me anything you like," he said, melting her anger with a sheepish grin.

Jenifer's laughter was a combination of relief and pent-up frustration. "I can think of *a lot* of things to call you."

She met his eyes in a long, loving look. The surprising thing was, he wasn't really fighting her on this. He did understand. His suggestion to meet in Dijon was a shot in the dark and he knew it. There was too much at stake to risk any involvement. It wasn't just that he was her teacher and that she cared so terribly much about what the others might think. She truly did not *want* to become involved with any man right now. She wanted her mind free to concentrate on herself, on her future. She could not think of love at a time like this, could not risk the emotional ups and downs that would be inevitable.

"Pierre, I told you a lot about myself when we were in Paris and . . . and when we had our picnic. But I'm not sure you understand how much this is costing me . . . this trip. And I don't mean just financially. I've left my sons. . . . I know what you told me about you and your mother and the separation being so important and all. But I'm all my sons have. They don't really have a father . . . not one who is there for them."

Pierre nodded understandingly.

"And I'm not telling you this so you'll give me any special consideration. This isn't a hard-luck story."

"I know that." He took her hand gently. "If your soufflé falls, you'll be treated just like anyone else."

Jen smiled at his feeble joke. "Of course I want to walk out of here with first prize, I want your finest recommendation so I can go back home and build a new life for myself. But what I need more than that is the knowledge that everything I get is because I deserve it."

"Am I face to face with the American Puritan Ethic?" Pierre smiled as he raised one of his heavy eyebrows.

Jen felt an erotic tug in her stomach as she looked at him. "Hardly that."

Pierre's dark eyes glistened with emotion and

he nodded. "Then we shall meet . . . strictly as friends."

Jen shook her head vehemently. "Do you realize that class of yours is like a school of piranhas? Do you realize they'll hate me if I'm even seen with you?"

"Aren't you exaggerating?" Pierre frowned.

"Pierre . . . I have to be honest. It's not just the other students. It's the wrong time for me. Maybe I'm scared . . . because of what happened in my marriage. But I didn't come to France to work out that part of my life. I need all my wits about me. It takes a lot of energy learning your language—that alone is draining. Although . . . as a matter of fact someone has already made a few suggestive remarks about us. I want to prove he's wrong."

Pierre pressed his lips together. "Albert Jamin. You went biking with him. I was jealous."

Jen smiled gently. "Well, don't be jealous."

"Damn it! This is ridiculous!" Pierre's dark eyes flashed, and for an instant she saw the other side of his nature, the reputedly angry, temperamental side.

"If you care about me," Jen said softly, "please . . . treat me the way you do the others."

"But I often lunch with my students," Pierre protested.

"I can't take a chance." Jen reached for the door handle and he stopped her. "Pierre, I'm not the sort of person who can function in a tense situation. I know myself well enough to know that if Albert and the others turn against me . . . I'll blow everything."

They looked at each other, their eyes glistening with a new passion, and in the silence the word "love" seemed to shimmer, unspoken.

"All right," Pierre nodded tightly.

"Good night," she murmured.

"Jen . . . let me drive you at least."

She shook her head. "Someone might be looking out the window at Madame Pauline's."

She climbed out of the car and turned back to him, feigning a brightness she did not feel. "By the way, I love Madame Pauline's . . . and her, too. It's going to be a good time for me, I know it is."

She walked briskly around the corner and cut across the street on a run. After a moment she heard his car start. He cruised at a safe distance behind her, pausing at the corner when she turned. He waited there until she opened the iron gate at Madame Pauline's and then she heard him drive on.

CHAPTER SIX

Was it possible that four and a half weeks had gone by since that first evening she had walked through Madame Pauline's garden? Jenifer pulled her plaid scarf around her neck and shoved her bare hands into the pockets of her brown corduroy jacket. She often sat on the little bench in Madame Pauline's garden late in the afternoon, after all of her classes were finished. Usually it helped. Usually the silence, the beauty of the few remaining roses, made it easier to finally climb the stairs to her room, where she generally spent the evening working on her French or studying one of the cookbooks borrowed from Pierre's Rennes's extensive library.

But tonight she was filled with such a sense of futility and regret that she could not bear the thought of going inside. The phone call to Duffy hadn't helped, either. It was always so difficult to time those infrequent calls home. Somehow today she got the time change all muddled and had called practically in the middle of the night. She had called because it was Mike's tenth birthday, but he had been so groggy that their talk had been unsatisfying.

Suddenly all the doubts that she had successfully staved off over the past month flooded in on her. Hadn't she deluded herself that a certificate from Pierre Rennes's school would change her life? What was it anyway but a scrap of paper? Could she have saved herself a lot of anguish by staying home?

"You out here, Jen?" Nellie Clyde emerged from inside on Edgard Moreau's arm. "Why don't you join us for dinner, dear?"

"Please . . ." Edgard touched her lightly on the shoulder. Over the past month he and Nellie had become inseparable.

Jen shook her head and smiled at them. They were the only members of the class whose attitude toward her was not cool and disdainful. Someone, and no doubt that someone was Albert, had circulated the rumor about her and Pierre.

"You're going to be the only person in history to return home from six weeks at La Petite Auberge thinner than when you arrived!" Nellie scolded her gently. "Jenifer, you've got to try some of these wonderful little restaurants up in the hill towns. We're all three on tight budgets and they're really quite reasonable." She cast a coy look at Edgard, who chuckled and hugged her arm tighter.

"We're a very international twosome." He winked at Jen. "We're not only French and English, but everywhere we go we insist on going dutch."

Nellie rolled her eyes and shook her head. "Edgard promises not to crack any jokes if you'll only join us."

Jen paused, considering. She really was loath to go inside and sit around feeling sorry for herself. But somehow she suspected that spending the evening with Nellie and Edgard, as much as she liked them, would not be the best thing for her ego. In her condition being a third wheel in the presence of two people who were obviously in love would only make matters worse.

"Saturday night." She put them off with a convincing grin. "I promise to join you then!"

She watched them go through the iron gate with a wistful expression on her face. Well, one positive thing was coming from all this. She was, as Nellie had pointed out, much thinner than when she'd arrived. Without trying, she had dropped eight pounds. At night, when she slipped beneath the icy sheets, her body felt as lithe as a child's. All her life she had imagined that being thin, seeing ever-so-slight hollows beneath her protruding cheekbones, would give her enormous pleasure. Only it didn't. At night, when she climbed into bed, she felt only the terrible ache of loneliness. Alone in the dark room, the strain of the three, sometimes five, hours spent in Pierre Rennes's presence finally took its toll. Most nights she tossed for an hour before finally turning on the light to read until the wee hours of the morning. Often it was almost dawn before she fell asleep. That she managed to remain alert and proficient in class amazed her. Perhaps the years of late-night feedings, the constant love and surveillance she had lavished on her children, had given her a stamina she had not known she possessed. She was a

woman who knew how to get through the day
. . . no matter what.

Only the night was another matter. During the
day she could ignore the sensation of his hand
placed casually on her shoulder as he watched her
perfect some culinary procedure. In front of the
others she could even laugh at his jokes, meet his
eyes without waivering, ask questions, respond—
in short, behave as if nothing unusual had passed
between them.

But the ordeal grew more painful with each
passing day because with every moment she grew
more passionately and deeply in love with him. A
month ago it was her body, her imagination, that
had been ensnared. But seeing him every day,
seeing his patience and even his sudden flares of
temper, she had come to respect him, to see the
whole man. She loved his wit, his brooding intensity, his absolute obsession with perfection.

Jenifer stood up and wandered slowly around
the rose garden trying to still the restlessness that
seized her body whenever darkness fell. It was
impossible to ignore the gossiping that was second
only to cooking as a pastime among the other students. She wondered if they didn't view her as
"the wounded party," an ambitious opportunist
who had made a play for the godlike Pierre's affec-
tions and lost. Lately the consensus seemed to be
that the languishing affair between Jeannete Du-
Bois and Pierre was bubbling with renewed vigor.

And then of course there was the huge oil painting of Catherine Rennes which hung over the fireplace in the after-dinner smoking room at the
Auberge. In it Catherine appeared like a blond
Amazon, dressed in formal riding attire, crop in
hand, her face haughty, proud, unsmiling and un-

101

deniably ravishing. Beneath the arresting portrait there was a little marker upon which the words "Madame Rennes" were scripted with a flourish. Whenever Jenifer passed it she felt herself shrivel into an insignificant speck. The portrait exuded the same power and sexuality that she felt from Pierre himself. Pierre and Catherine, the perfect match.

Jen closed her eyes, trying to shake off thoughts of him. She wasn't the least bit hungry. They had nibbled on Pierre's delicate quenelles all afternoon. But maybe a walk would help and perhaps a cup of coffee at the little pastry shop on the square.

Two more weeks left, only two. She wondered why she didn't look forward to the end, since each day seemed to be more difficult. It was too confusing. One minute she would be dying to leave, would actually entertain thoughts of quitting and returning home to her boys and all the familiar, predictable aspects of life in Duffy. At those moments life in Duffy seemed unbearably sweet and perfect. But then the next minute she would be seized with an impetuous, wild, stormy feeling, viewing her former life as a trap and herself as a plump, spineless victim. At those moments she would know, beyond a shadow of a doubt, that she could never again settle for living a life where she had so little control.

But how much control did she have now, if all she could do was spend every night trying to steer her thoughts away from Pierre Rennes? She dismissed the bothersome question with an impatient toss of her hair.

For the first time it occurred to her that Nellie was right, she *was* missing out on the greatest opportunity of all by not visiting some of the small out-of-the-way restaurants for which the area was famous. After all, if she was serious about eventually opening her own place, such information could prove invaluable. The French were as famous for their small, unpretentious, inexpensive restaurants as they were for the opulent three-star varieties. If she stayed in the Duffy vicinity she would certainly gravitate toward a homey place that specialized in the hearty stews of Burgundy.

From this moment on, she told herself, she was through nursing her wounds like a lovesick adolescent. She would try to appreciate the opportunities around her.

"I've been looking for you." Jen looked up as Eric Martin stepped outside. "I'm about to drive up to Meursault to a spot that's supposed to serve the best *coq au vin* in the region. How about joining me?"

"I stuffed myself on quenelles . . ." Jen caught herself and laughed. Here she was already trying to weasel out of the promise she'd made herself. "Give me a minute," she cried as she ran inside to put on her coat.

"I'll give you two," Eric called after her.

Well, at least she wasn't having dinner with her *least* favorite man in the class and at least he spoke English so she wouldn't have to exert all her mental energy trying to come up with the right gender.

Even in the dark the drive up to the hilltop village was lovely and she found herself honestly enjoying Eric's company. Although their backgrounds couldn't have been more different, they were both Americans and for the moment that seemed to draw them together. For once Eric was not trying to impress her with all the glamorous details of his life in his Chicago penthouse apartment. He asked about her life in Duffy, about her children, and wondered what her plans were when she returned home. He even admitted to being just a bit homesick.

The highly touted *coq au vin* exceeded all of her expectations. "And I said I wasn't hungry!" she laughed as she ran a crust of bread around the rim of her plate to sop up the last residue of the hearty wine sauce.

Eric reached for the bottle of Beaujolais, which was nearly empty.

"No more for me." Jen's cheeks were flushed from so much wine.

"One more bottle." Eric motioned to the old woman who owned the place.

"You're kidding!" Jen cast him a dubious look.

". . . and some cheese and fruit," he called after her.

"Eric, you're going to be drinking that entire bottle yourself." Jen smiled. A warning signal went off inside her head but it was offset by the sense of well-being engendered by the wine and the dinner. "And I'm going to drive home," she added lightly as he sampled the new bottle.

Jen watched him swirl the red liquid around in his glass before drinking it. He had been pleasant all evening, but suddenly he seemed tense, almost hostile.

"So what will you be making for the final competition?" He eyed her suspiciously.

Surely he couldn't have invited her out to dinner just to lure that piece of information out of her? Jen shook her head and shrugged. She honestly didn't know what she would cook.

"I overheard Albert say that he was going to do

104

an entire five-course meal." Eric gave a cynical laugh.

"Good luck to Albert." Jen raised her empty wineglass in a good-natured toast. Eric had drunk far too much, but she knew better than to suggest he stop.

"Don't you want to know what I'm going to make?" He raised a flirtatious eyebrow.

Jen laughed, determined to treat the situation lightly. "We're not supposed to tell."

"Childish, don't you think?" Eric gave her a sharp look, then gulped down the rest of his wine.

"Maybe," Jen agreed. "But it's the way Monsieur Rennes has arranged things."

"Monsieur Rennes!" Eric overenunciated and mimicked a supercilious attitude, which Jen guessed was supposed to indicate his impression of Pierre. "If we were all to tell each other what we were cooking for Monsieur Rennes's ridiculous contest, there would be no hush-hush secret."

"That's true." Jen nibbled nervously on a crust of bread. Eric was determined to pick a fight.

"You don't find the whole thing absurd?" he asked harshly.

Jen met his angry blue eyes with a candid smile. "Eric, there's been a cloak and dagger quality to everything since we arrived. I've never been to any other cooking schools in France. But Nellie swears they're all the same. Has something to do with Gallic intensity."

"Like hell it does!" Eric pushed his chair back, making a loud scraping noise, which caused the other diners to turn and stare.

"It's not that serious." Jen touched his arm.

"I'll tell you something." He hunched forward with a conspiratorial smile. "Monsieur Rennes is

105

one of the most overrated chefs in France. I'm not the only one who thinks so."

"You're entitled to your opinion," Jen said steadily.

"Why, thank you," Eric replied archly. "But what is your opinion?"

Jen paused, trying to evaluate the best course of action.

"But then," Eric went on, "Monsieur Rennes is a handsome fellow, so perhaps that accounts for some of his popularity with the ladies."

Jen gave him a sharp look. It was the liquor, she told herself, and again she reminded herself not to let him arouse her anger.

"The truth is, my dear Jenifer, winner of the Bradley Bake-off, that your Monsieur Rennes would have amounted to nothing without his ex-wife's money and name to support his meager little talent."

Jen clasped her hands together beneath the table. "Eric, Michelin does not dole out three stars to a restaurant without good reason."

"People can always be bought." Eric grew pensive. It seemed to Jen that he was speaking from personal experience.

"Have you eaten at La Petite Auberge?" he asked resentfully.

"It's not in my budget," Jen replied tightly. She was fast losing patience.

"Well, how can you speak with so much authority?" he accused. "I have eaten there. Three times. And each time I was dismally disappointed. Oh, of course, the service was all very grand. Nobody outdoes the French when it comes to the pomp and circumstance of dining. But it's all gloss, all show. Classical cuisine with a *nouveau* twist! Boring! The sauces on both the veal dishes were so bland I couldn't identify any of the ingredients. I mean, face it, Jenifer, you're in the course, you know what I'm talking about." He paused, waiting for her affirmation. "You're afraid to admit it because that will mean you've wasted a lot of time and money, huh? That's why none of the others will admit that the great master chef has several large and *tasteless* flaws."

"Eric, do you mind if we change the subject?" Jen interjected with as much pleasantness as she could summon.

"All he has is technique," he went on thoughtlessly. "I'll give him that. But technique is not what makes a chef. *Taste* is. Hell, I'm a better chef. For that matter, you are, too. . . . I'm not kidding." Eric scowled. "The man has no taste, no imagination. Cooking is one of the last of the great sensual arts and . . ."

"Eric, I really don't see the point," Jen finally bristled. She glanced at her watch and reached into her purse for some money. "My share."

Eric scooped up the bills without a word and rose to pay the check. Thank heavens he had not put up a fuss about leaving the unfinished bottle of wine. She complimented the proprietress and went outside to wait for Eric.

The stars were bright and the ancient town square was flooded with moonlight. Back home in Duffy they called it a harvest moon. She'd have to remember to ask Edgard what the French equivalent was.

Poor Eric. Now that she had extricated herself from what might have been an embarrassing situation, she felt sorry for him. He was always bragging, always trying to gain the approval of his

107

classmates. Really, he was very insecure. Putting two and two together, she concluded he was indeed the proverbial poor little rich boy. No doubt his family had staked him to his fancy restaurant. Perhaps underneath it all, he was terribly unsure of his talents and sought to bolster his ego through his constant boasting.

"I'm glad we came." Jen smiled gently as he helped her into the car, but his sullen expression did not change.

Eric slammed the car door and sat tautly behind the wheel. Then, without warning, he turned to Jen, took her in his arms and kissed her.

"Eric!" She struggled away from him, shocked.

"I love you," he blurted out as he clasped her roughly against his tense body.

For a moment Jen was too astonished to do anything but cling to him. He had flirted openly with her during the first two weeks but she had assumed her continued rejections had dampened his interest. It must be the wine, she thought. The wine was making him act this way. As his mouth sought hers again she squirmed out of the embrace.

Rather than risk more awkwardness or another futile exchange of words, Jen opened the door and slid out of the car. "Don't worry about me, Eric. I'll find my way home."

She turned and walked rapidly back across the square, praying that he would elect to pay her back by leaving her stranded. A moment later she heard him gun the motor of his Renault. She held her breath as he raced the car once around the square, shattering the calm stillness of the night. Poor Eric. He had had so much to drink, he would never even remember this awful scene tomorrow!

Jen stood listening as the angry sound of Eric's car grew fainter until the night was once again blissfully silent.

She could always phone Nellie. Edgard would be happy to drive out and pick her up. She looked up at the stars and after a moment crossed to the center of the square. She sat on the edge of an old stone fountain whose waters had long since ceased to flow. She breathed in the cool evening air, closing her eyes.

After a few minutes, Jen shook herself out of her peaceful reverie. It was already past ten and if she was going to phone Nellie she should do it right away. But she was reluctant to leave the peaceful, sleepy village and she continued sitting on the edge of the fountain, drinking in the frigid air, observing the few men who came and left the cheerfully lighted bar next to the church. Maybe she would spend the night here. Yes, tomorrow was Saturday and there were no classes. A night away from Madame Pauline's might be just what she needed.

On impulse she ventured into the one very modest hotel. To her delight the rooms were very reasonable. The concierge, a sleepy-eyed young matron, handed her a key and directed her to a narrow back stairway. Her room turned out to be a charming garret with low, beamed ceilings and windows overlooking the cobblestone square. Jen sat on the freshly made bed, looking out into the crystalline night and feeling an unparalleled sense of freedom. She had no nightgown, no toothbrush, no book, no other person to talk to or consult with and yet for the first time in weeks she did not feel lonely.

But neither could she seriously entertain

thoughts of sleep. She was seized with an eager restlessness, an excitement. Suddenly she could truly see herself as the proprietress of her own establishment. She had learned an enormous amount from Pierre, not the least of which was his flawless sense of style, the simplicity with which he presented his food. She pulled her coat back on, tiptoed downstairs and went back outside.

She would start small. Duffy was not a high rent area and she could probably find something for very little money. And she would use all of the tips she had learned here. The only restaurants in the Duffy vicinity were either fast-food places or sprawling dark motel-type places that served steaks, roast beef and fried chicken. She would specialize in simple peasant cuisine—stews redolent with wine and herbs, unique but elegant salads on which one could make a whole meal.

She wandered around the village, dreaming of her restaurant. Perhaps there would only be eight tables like the restaurant where she and Eric had dined. The attic in her parents' house was full of old linens. Great-grandmother Morely's lace curtains were there. She could use them, and then, of course, she would fill the place with fresh flowers, in the French style.

For the first time she was able to grapple with specifics. If she could find a place for $200 a month, and she was almost positive she could, she could fix it up for around $2,000 (including a used stove, refrigerator, dishwasher, etc.) and with an additional $2,000 she could be in business. She would aim for $5,000. Up until now she had lacked the confidence to even consider asking anyone to lend her that kind of money. Now she knew she could make a go of her own business. She knew a couple of people who had that kind of money to lend and she would write them all tomorrow!

She retraced her steps and arrived back at the town square just as the tower clock struck eleven thirty. The low hum of a car cut through the silence and Jen turned in time to see Pierre Rennes's yellow Citroën pull up in front of the bar.

Her first impulse was to dart back into the alleyway. She was certain he would be with Jeannete and she braced herself to meet them.

"Mon Dieu!" Stepping out of the car, Pierre stopped in his tracks as if he were seeing a ghost.

He was alone. Jen tried to think of something casual to say but her mind was a blank. She was aware only of the warmth of his eyes and that they were alone in front of the little medieval church.

"The last person you expected to see, right?" Jen found her voice first.

Pierre nodded, still staring in disbelief. A warm thrill coursed through her body as she realized the unmistakable impact her presence was having on him.

"What are you doing here?" He moved toward her and took her by both arms, looking at her closely, intensely, as if checking to see if she was hurt.

"I'm all right," Jen assured him, shaken by his proximity. He had not looked at her that way since their last night together.

"You're sure?" He bent his head close to hers. She could feel his breath, warm and faltering. "Jenifer . . . ?" He tilted her chin upward with one hand and feasted hungrily on her face.

Crazy erotic sensations were already tumbling uncontrollably inside her. Her mouth was moist with longing. Now they were no longer strangers.

111

For four long weeks they had held their feelings in abeyance but now all barriers were down. She felt herself drowning in his torrid gaze. No, she did not want to break away. Her body craved his touch now more than ever.

"Do you feel it, too?" Pierre brought his mouth within inches of hers. "Chance has brought us together a second time."

"Yes." Jen smiled softly, heady with longing. She wanted him. She would abandon herself to his every desire. Tonight. Nothing else mattered.

"I love you." He breathed the words against her yielding mouth, taking her in a kiss of such infinite gentleness that she was overcome by dizziness and clung to him.

I love you. The words reverberated inside her head as his wayward hands caressed her. He loved her? He had murmured the words and she could not remember if he had spoken them in French or in English. She kissed him back with a passion that mounted with each fiery stroke of her tongue. Could not remember which language? She was seized by a wild feeling of giddiness, which compelled her to wrap her arms around his neck even tighter.

"Je t'aime," she thrilled as he wound his arms around her supple diminutive body. The night was magic.

Beneath the crystalline star-sprinkled sky, he murmured, "I love you!" His eyes were moist with longing. Jen caressed his stubbly cheek with tears in her eyes.

"Je t'aime . . ." she answered in French without even thinking.

CHAPTER SEVEN

Suddenly they were laughing. With tears streaming down their cheeks, they stood in the middle of the deserted village collapsing against each other as if the past four weeks had been the buildup to this extraordinary revelation.

"I knew you loved me!" Pierre whisked Jen off the ground and for a minute she thought he intended to hurl her playfully up into the magical heavens. "I knew you did!" He placed her carefully back down on the ground as if suddenly aware of his own strength, of her delicate body.

"I didn't know you did." Jen sank against him, wrapping her arms around him and feeling the delicious arousal begin to grow.

"What are you doing here?" Pierre rocked her back and forth. "Come, let's go in for a brandy, yes? This is a long overdue celebration!"

But before she could take a step, his arms were around her and he was devouring her in another sensual kiss.

"One brandy, no? And then . . . ?" He smiled

devilishly. "The appetizer always makes the main course more satisfying," he teased as they entered the deserted bar.

"Alfonse!" Pierre greeted the old man behind the bar with a wave. "Why are you here?" he asked as she slid into one of the little booths.

"Why are *you* here?" she asked, feasting on his strong angular face. Just looking at him stirred her to a near feverish pitch.

"Does it matter?" he laughed. "It only matters that we are. And together!"

He clasped her hands exuberantly, so different from their last painful encounter the night she told him they could no longer meet. This was different. Tonight they were meeting . . . as equals. Something had changed in her over the past month. She had a new confidence, a new sense of self, and for the first time in her life she had a vision for her own future. Her eyes sparkled as she basked in his adoring gaze. She was no longer afraid.

"Merci." Pierre thanked the old man, who had come with the brandy. He handed Jenifer a glass and lifted his own to his lips. The dynamic attraction was even more intense, but now there was an ease, an acceptance, which bound them in a new, thrilling intimacy.

"To us." Pierre's dark eyes smoldered with a sensual promise as explicit as the touch of his hand on her breast. A powerful longing swelled inside her but now she savored the agonizing sensation.

"Do you know what it means to find you here?" Pierre asked after a moment. "Do you know how rare this is? This village . . . how did you get here?" He interrupted himself, laughing, then continued his explanation in a burst of enthusiasm.

114

"Meursault is very precious to me. It is my favorite village. The only regret I have about La Petite Auberge is that it is not located in Meursault. For years I have been coming up to Alfonse's bar when I finish work, but lately . . . certain pressures have precluded my visits. Tonight, for the first time in weeks, I decided to treat myself kindly and drive up. And who do I see, before even I stop my car?"

He raised his heavy eyebrows and widened his eyes in an exaggerated expression of astonishment.

"Me!" Jenifer thrilled to the wild, erotic sensations that ravaged her. "Me," she repeated in a whisper, and once again they sat in trancelike silence.

"I came up for dinner." She smiled, surrendering to the spell he cast over her. "I decided not to go back . . ."

"Ever . . . ?" Pierre listened with the entranced expression she remembered so well.

Jen laughed. "No"—she indulged his fantasy— "not ever. I decided to remain up here in the medieval clouds for the rest of my life."

"It's a rare spot," Pierre acknowledged fondly. "One of the best-kept secrets. When I'm here I feel content. I can think things out when I'm here.

"And of course"—he grinned—"the brandy also helps."

"Yes!" Jen enthused. "I feel the same way about Meursault. . . . I came up here this evening, more out of a sense of obligation than because I was really interested in coming. I thought it was about time I ventured out of my cocoon, saw some of the sights. And . . . and then I found myself sitting on that little fountain in the square, think-

115

ing more clearly than I have in my life. Pierre, when I go back home . . . I'm going to open my own restaurant!"

Her newly formed plan bubbled out and she embellished on it, encouraged by the light in Pierre's eye. He understood how important her excitement was, that it was, most importantly, a manifestation of her newly acquired confidence, a sense of herself and her own remarkable potential. He not only listened attentively, he made suggestions based on his own experience. Dimly she was aware that implicit in her exciting new plan was a separation from him. Duffy was in Iowa, La Petite Auberge was in Burgundy. But at the moment that seemed irrelevant. The intimacy she felt with Pierre, their extraordinary bond insulated her from all doubts, all fears.

He cared about what she wanted! For the first time in her life she was dreaming, out loud, to a man and he wasn't ignoring her or chastising her for being unrealistic.

"You've had quite an evening meandering around the streets of Meursault, devising your scheme. I think it sounds good, Jen. You'll get the money to finance it."

"I want it badly, Pierre," she told him earnestly.

He nodded. "That's why you'll get it."

"People don't always get what they want," Jen sighed, but her eyes continued to radiate a growing sense of confidence.

"But they get what they need," he said thoughtfully. "At least I think that is true. And I think you need this. You need it more than in the financial sense. You need to make something all your own."

"Something small," Jen rhapsodized. "I would want it to stay small."

116

"I hope that is not a criticism of L'Auberge," Pierre teased.

"No, no!" Jen rushed on. "It's just that part of my vision is that it will remain small. That's not to say I don't want the business to grow. And I know how the business can grow and the restaurant stay small!"

"The rare air of Meursault has unleashed the soul of a mogul!"

Jen laughed. "Maybe. Anyhow it's not an original idea but I think it's appropriate for what I have in mind and for the vicinity surrounding Duffy. I will use the restaurant as headquarters, as a little mecca out of which a mail-order gourmet business operates! I don't mean in the beginning. But if it all takes off."

"Is this the same young woman who thought she could negotiate with a Paris waiter because she'd gone off without her money?"

"You will never let me forget that, will you?" Jen laughed happily.

"No." Pierre smiled. "You learn quickly, however. You know you are my best student."

"Well . . ."

"Don't protest." Pierre took her hand and rubbed the tips of her fingers lightly over his soft, full lips. Jen closed her eyes briefly with a sigh. He regarded her with an enigmatic smile and then continued. "I have been above reproach in keeping my promise to you. I have shown no partiality and have resisted every temptation to play the ogre. The many times late at night when I have had the urge to telephone you, I have resisted. It has not been easy."

"I know." Jen felt a rush of emotion as their eyes met. She squeezed his hand.

117

"Shall we go?" The invitation unleashed a hot surge inside her. "My house is very near . . . but suddenly it seems too far."

"We don't have to go that far." Jen's pulse quickened to a maddening speed. "If it's all right with you . . . I'd just as soon go across the street to the Relais Meursault. I've booked a room there."

Pierre gave a low chuckle. "Another surprise. Well, I've always wondered what it would be like to live in Meursault." He reached into his pocket and withdrew his leather wallet. "Excuse me one moment while I pay Alfonse." He extracted a bill and walked over to the bar, leaving his wallet open on the table. Several cards and papers slipped out and she reached over to tuck them back inside so he would not lose them. Then a photograph caught her eye. She drew in her breath abruptly. The smiling face of Catherine Rennes stared up at her from inside the wallet.

Jenifer averted her eyes instantly, as if she could erase the image of the radiantly beautiful Catherine from her mind. Suddenly she felt deceived.

Of course he had not forgotten Catherine Rennes. Who could forget such an intriguing, beautiful woman? And who was Jen beside such a woman? She cringed remembering how she had rambled on about her idea of opening a modest restaurant. Catherine Rennes had won Academy Awards, her picture was constantly on the cover of one magazine or another. In her thirty-some years she had probably amassed a small fortune.

No wonder Pierre had seemed so nonplussed about Jen's return to the States to open a restaurant. Suddenly the risk of being with him was too great, the price far too high. The bewildering complexity she had sensed from him in the begin-

118

ning surfaced again with even greater vehemence.

Jen followed him out of Alfonse's in a daze, Catherine's smiling face haunting her.

"What is the matter?" He stopped midway across the square and looked down at her.

If only she could ignore the question, plunge blindly ahead and live with her regrets tomorrow. If only . . .

"Jenifer . . . ?"

She felt lost, completely miserable and defeated. Had she misjudged him so terribly? Could he have lied so blatantly, so easily? None of it made sense. But she no longer trusted him. Whatever secret he kept locked inside himself had festered there too long.

"What is it?" he repeated.

"I think this is a mistake," Jen articulated finally.

"Why the sudden change?" She felt him stiffen. "Dammit, you cannot change your mind like that!"

Jen ignored his anger and walked stonily toward the Relais. The village of Meursault presented such a peaceful, idyllic face to the world. She had deluded herself that life could be the same.

He stepped in front of her, blocking her way. "You can't turn off that way after what happened between us tonight!"

"Oh, yes I can," Jen felt suddenly weak. She sank slowly down and sat on the steps of the Relais. "Are you still in love with Catherine?" She asked, not looking at him but staring straight ahead.

"Catherine?"

The way he growled the name sent a chill up her spine. She glanced at his face. It was twisted

119

into a bitter smile that distorted his features. He did not look like the same man.

"In love with Catherine?" He raised his voice, filling the peaceful square with an eerie laugh.

"Oh, no!" He turned abruptly and sank down on the steps beside her. "Oh, no, I do not *love* Catherine. I despise Catherine, as anyone who truly knows me will tell you."

He drew in a deep breath to steady himself.

"Why are you asking this now?" he asked harshly.

"Why do you carry her picture in your wallet? I saw it there."

"Ah . . ." His defiant expression softened. He reached for her hand but she pulled away. "I keep it there as a reminder," he told her, regaining some of the fierceness he had exhibited when she first mentioned his ex-wife.

"I don't understand." Jen felt no relief in hearing that he did not love Catherine Rennes. That he could hate anyone so fiercely was little comfort.

"I'm sorry you saw Catherine's picture," he said in a composed voice. "Since you did . . . I suppose it sounds peculiar . . . I'm not proud of it but . . . for the moment I keep Catherine's picture with me as a reminder to go slow, to look beneath the surface and consider more than superficial appearances."

How could she respond? Jen felt his arm around her shoulder but she could do nothing but look blankly out across the cobblestoned square. He was still obsessed with Catherine, even if all his thoughts were negative ones. Catherine Rennes owned him. And who was she to compete with such great passion?

"Pierre . . ." She tried to get up but he pulled

120

her gently against his broad chest. For a moment she allowed herself to sink into him, to feel again all of the yearning he inspired in her. She felt his hands sifting through her thick tangle of red hair and knew by the rapid movement of his chest how much he wanted her.

"Nothing has changed between us," he murmured as his mouth sought hers.

His kiss was all fire, like ragged bolts of lightning, sharp and fierce and deadly. But where would it all lead? She felt ravaged, torn between the agonizing ecstasy he promised and the stupefying remorse which was sure to follow.

"No!" She twisted out of his arms and raced up the stairs into the Relais. One small lamp burned on the small reception desk and she found her way to the narrow stairway with its help. Upstairs she let herself into her room, alone in the darkness.

She wanted not to think, wanted to shriek for the injustice of it all. She had had such a simple life in Duffy. She had been placid, free of desire, passionless.

Quickly undressing, she wrapped a worn white quilt around her naked body and tiptoed over to the window. The Relais had been dark and quiet for hours. In all likelihood she was the only guest. But the feeling that she was on dangerous ground would not abate. She stood at the side of the window, pulled the curtain aside and looked down on the square. Pierre's yellow Citroën was still there. She squinted to see if he was inside.

Her breath was coming in shallow, quick pants, as if she had been running. She flung herself onto the bed, knowing that sleep was out of the question. Her body was still throbbing from his touch.

121

It seemed that nothing would still the tormenting desire he had awakened in her.

She moved again to the window, praying that he had driven off without her hearing. But no, the Citroën remained stubbornly in its place in front of Alfonse's bar.

A soft knock at her door sent the hot blood shooting through her. How could he have found her? She stood frozen next to the window. He did not knock again but she felt his presence on the other side of the door, felt his virility intruding upon her solitude.

Jenifer crossed slowly to the door and opened it, lowering her eyes as Pierre stepped inside. His huge form dominated the tiny room. He ducked his head in order to avoid the low beams and Jen turned away, feeling her trembling, naked body beneath the white quilt. She stared out the window, unseeing, and her breathing accelerated as she heard the rustle of clothes as Pierre undressed.

A moment later he was behind her, running his hands along her bare shoulders. Without a word she dropped the quilt and he pressed his powerful body into her firm, well-shaped behind. For several seconds they stood mesmerized by the first electrifying connection.

Slowly he began to move back and forth in a provocative motion. His hands massaged the back of her neck, releasing the accumulated tension. His sensitive prodding of those tight muscles spoke to her deeply and her body stirred in readiness. A breeze caressed the front of her naked body and her breasts stiffened, eager for his touch. As he manipulated the muscles along her back she felt herself giving way to erotic sensations. Finally feeling his burgeoning desire against her buttocks, she could no longer stifle her impatience. She whirled to face him, pressing full against him as his mouth came down hard and hungry on hers.

The kiss, a tempestuous struggle, left them breathless. Pierre held her at arm's length, his eyes blazing into hers. The heat of his gaze as it traveled the length of her nude body made her weak with longing. She forced herself to stand there, feeling his eyes penetrate her femininity.

Gaining courage, she tore her eyes from the breadth of his shoulders to the dark mass of coarse hair on his chest, down to his taut abdomen and lower still. Although they were no longer touching, their ragged breathing fell into a measured rhythm, propelling them to greater erotic heights. She was no longer thinking. Her body trembled in the moonlight and she knew she had never seen anything as astoundingly virile, as beautiful, as Pierre Rennes.

He moved slowly toward her until their bodies touched and she felt him stirring against her. Her breasts flattened into his chest, nipples hardening at his touch. Jen closed her eyes as he inched his heavy muscular thigh between her bare legs. He moved it slowly back and forth, driving her to the brink of ecstasy. The tempo he set was demonically slow and sensual. There would be no rushing here. She felt each sensation with an almost painful clarity. She was not accustomed to so much . . . so much pleasure. When his mouth sought hers and his tongue shot fire inside her, a small shudder shook her.

He lowered her onto the bed and stood for several moments gazing down on her pale prone body, the full breasts and tiny waist curving into luscious firm hips. She closed her eyes, aware only of his intense scrutiny and how fully he aroused her even when they were not touching. With each passing second her desire mounted until, in a near state of torment, she drew herself to him, clasping his powerful waist.

Nothing like this had ever happened to her before. Nor had she dreamed it. She buried her head in him, reveling in his clean masculine smell, bombarded by so many new evocative sensations that her head reeled. Her hands explored the small of his back, the tight muscularity of his behind and the slender loins—all so different from her own yielding, curvaceous body.

Her fingers roamed over him, fascinated. She kissed him, hugging him closer and closer in a frenzied attempt to know all of him. She felt his large hands massaging her shoulders, urging her, dispelling the last of her hesitancy.

"My love . . ." She scarcely heard his deep erotic moan, for she was lost in him, oblivious to everything but the feel of him. Her tongue moved over him, propelling him into the same agonizing state in which she was lost.

"Jenifer!" Her mouth left him, and he fell down on the bed next to her. His control was shattered. His hands flew over her body, titillating her with a demonic tenderness that left her gasping. Following her lead, he parted her legs, nuzzling into her, driving her to near madness with his warm breath. She writhed in a mindless ecstasy as his tongue swirled and dipped. She was a heartbeat, one singular throbbing passionate heartbeat clinging to a man who was as dear to her as life itself. A series of warm convulsions shook her and she arched toward him to let him know she was ready for him.

Pierre poised over her and for a fraction of a

second their eyes met. Then his weight, the longed-for, breathtaking sensation of his body covered her.

He gripped her hips, guiding her into another unknown, uncharted land. How was it possible that he knew each rhythm she craved? He twisted to one side, then to the other, and she followed him as if she lived inside his body. He drove her higher, harder and with an almost frightening intensity.

The cataclysmic encounter built to a new crescendo as Pierre's driving rhythm grew more turbulent. His passion knew no bounds. Each time she exploded he was challenged to offer her more, breathing her name, inflaming her with sultry French words whose meanings she could only dimly guess. His hunger for her seemed insatiable. In one quick movement he lifted her up and rolled over until she lay on top of his chest. She opened her mouth and kissed him deeply, acknowledging the pleasure he gave her and urging him with the slow circular movement of her hips to take the moment for himself.

How was it possible to love this man so much? Jen abandoned herself to his final journey. She wanted to give him everything, and from deep within herself she established a pace which in contrast to his wild unbridled rhythm was exquisitely slow and languid. Jen watched his face as she led him, and his pleasure was a narcotic to her. When his moment came she was there.

She collapsed against his heaving chest and they lay spent, floating in the aftermath of their lovemaking. Pierre stroked her head, soothing her until her breathing grew easier and her lips parted in a peaceful smile and she fell blissfully asleep.

In the middle of the night she awoke to find him sucking gently on one nipple, his hand trailing tenderly up her inner thigh. She half opened her eyes, gave him a languid smile and abandoned herself to his nocturnal pleasure.

"You don't have to do anything," he murmured as he caressed her. "You can go back to sleep."

Her smile broadened at the thought of sleep. She was already alive and tingling. His fingers, penetrating into her darkness, were flooding her with light. She surrendered to the poetry of their movement and yielded to the soft erotic sound of his mouth as it played languidly around her nipple. The night was magic after all. She buried her hands in his thick dark hair and half closed her eyes. But in a matter of minutes she could no longer tolerate the divine ecstasy. She was straining and ready. Unabashedly she led him to the source of his desire.

She dug her fingers into his broad heaving back and arched into him, wrapping her legs around him with renewed vigor. She felt as if she had been born again. The power and energy he unleashed in her seemed to be infinite.

Their bodies moved together in a surge of erotic urgency as their lips met and they continued their tireless exploration. On and on they pitched from peak to peak, clinging to each other as if each taste only increased their hunger. Jen ran her tongue, pink and moist, around his searching mouth. The boldness she felt in his arms was nothing less than miraculous.

"For so many nights I have imagined how I would make love to you . . . all night." Pierre rained kisses on her face as he accelerated his dizzying tempo. "It is even better than I dreamed."

He burned a long deep kiss into her and she felt the flames leaping through her body.

They slept again, nestled in each other's arms, damp and smiling. But once again sleep was only a brief respite.

"An interlude." Pierre kissed her awake for the third time. "An interlude between courses," he teased.

Jen laughed as she lay sprawled on the disheveled bed, her red hair wild and flowing onto the pillow.

"You are so beautiful." Pierre touched the tip of her chin tenderly, then leaned down and rubbed his cheek against hers. "It will be dawn in one hour."

"What does that mean?" Jen smiled languidly.

"It means that we will be daylight lovers." He eased himself between her legs and took her smoothly, with a serenity of movement that plunged them both into a deep, dreamless sleep.

When Jen woke next the room was flooded with bright sunlight and Pierre was sitting fully dressed on the side of the bed, staring down at her. The sight of him brought on a rush of mixed feelings. She grabbed the sheet and drew it up around her breasts, recalling her audacious behavior of the night before.

But what an infantile response that was. She chided herself silently and flung the covers aside. She looked around uncertainly for her clothes, trying to think of something appropriate to say. She looked back at Pierre, who was watching her with a bemused smile.

"You regret it all," he said lowly. "I know. You wish it had never happened."

Jen met his smiling eyes, feeling the panic rise

and fall. At the same time she felt that delicious erotic twirling in her stomach and she flopped back down onto her pillow overcome with memories of last night's lovemaking. Now what? Now they were lovers. She was practically catatonic with panic. At the same time her body was singing. She was already craving him. She sneaked a quick look in his direction and saw that he was waiting patiently with the same bemused expression.

All right, so he had read her mind. He had guessed that any woman who would believe a Paris waiter would accept an IOU would also experience a certain amount of doubt and uneasiness the "morning after." He probably also knew that the only other man she had ever made love to was her former husband.

"No one will know." He kissed her lightly, still smiling.

Jen felt a little smile playing on her mouth. Beneath the covers she pressed her legs together and felt a warm thrill shoot through her body. Outside the square was alive with early morning activity. And he said no one would know?

Suddenly her panic escalated and she turned away, clutching her pillow. She had jeopardized everything by mixing business with pleasure. And just when she had been so close. Oh, she didn't delude herself that there could be any real future with him but . . .

He turned her around firmly, interrupting her panicky thoughts. "Please. You must not do this to yourself. You are so unaccustomed to feeling pleasure, you must not now regret. I love you. I want only your happiness. I know what you are thinking. But I proved to you before that you could trust me and I will not let you down."

Jenifer drew in a long breath and raised her brown eyes reluctantly. He was right. She was not accustomed to feeling pleasure. When she was with him she was happy. She wasn't used to being happy with a man.

"When you left me outside last night"—he drew the sheet chastely over her breasts—"I stood for some time in the street thinking about my motives with you and about the many mistakes I have made in love. I did not want to behave blindly, as I so often have in the past."

"You knew I would feel guilty?" Jen whispered.

Pierre brushed a lock of red hair off her forehead, "Let's say I was prepared for the possibility."

"But . . ." Jen felt an erotic shiver run through her. "I'm not a prude, am I?" She gave him an impish smile and he laughed.

"You are the woman of my dreams!" He wrestled her around playfully and planted an ardent kiss on her pliant mouth. "You will soon become accustomed to all kinds of pleasures. You don't have to pay for everything, Jenifer."

His face was stubbly from want of a shave but the slightly abrasive sensation only made her want him more. She snuggled toward him seductively, inviting him with her soft, yielding kisses, tantalizing him with her body, which lay exposed and trembling with impatience in the morning light. As long as he was kissing her, as long as she felt the warmth of his masculinity, the conflict which raged in her was stilled. It was too soon to be filled with doubts. Too soon to question the future. He stripped quickly and joined her, caressing her and stroking her as if he understood that only the eloquence of his touch could banish her uneasiness.

"You must give yourself . . . and *me* . . . this day," he crooned softly after they had made love.

Jen nodded. Rationally she knew that he was right. She reached out to touch the taut skin beneath his rib cage. She sat back and watched as he dressed. Of course he was right. It had been her decision as well as his to surrender to passion and now she would have to rise above her fears.

She stood up and began to dress, feeling his eyes on her as she moved about the tiny room gathering up her clothes. Wasn't she just afraid to let herself feel really happy? So much of her life dealt with logistics, plans, puzzling out the intricacies of the next moment for herself and her sons. He was right when he said she wasn't used to taking the moment for herself. And what did she expect after one night anyway? A proposal?

She winced at the thought, recognizing that somewhere deep inside her lay the old adage about what it meant to be a decent woman. But of course she wasn't going to marry Pierre Rennes. She had known that from the start, so what was the point in dragging out that burdensome piece of old morality?

"You are thinking again," he addressed her in French, then repeated himself in English.

"I understood!" Jen whirled around smiling. "Pierre! You didn't slow down for me and I understood. Let's speak French all day? All right?"

Pierre helped her into her coat. "If it helps you not to think those negative thoughts."

Jen turned to him, laughing, and replied in French, "No more thinking . . . only talking.

130

And in French! And"—she broke down momentarily and spoke English as he helped her into his car—"since I'm just starting on the future tense . . . no more talking about the future!"

CHAPTER EIGHT

"I will take you to one of my favorite spots," Pierre said, putting down the top to the convertible. Jen felt the warm October sun beating down on her head as it had during their first drive together from Paris to Beaune. "The best coffee in Burgundy and the most unusual setting," he added with a devilish glint in his eye.

"But you have to work." Jen glanced at the clock on the dashboard and saw that it was almost noon. They didn't even have class on Saturday morning because Saturday was such a busy luncheon day at the Auberge.

"Ah ha!" Pierre stuck his forefinger playfully into her ribs and wiggled it.

"Pierre!" Jen squirmed away, laughing. "You have to work, don't you?"

"Ah ha!" Pierre repeated, and accelerated the motor so that the car bumped a bit crazily over some railroad tracks. His dark eyes danced as he looked at her and it dawned on her that she had not seen that relaxed expression on his face once during the past month.

I love you, Pierre . . . the words reverberated inside her head and echoed in her body. She reached over and patted his shoulder fondly, enjoying the carefree, easy sense of friendship that had overtaken them since checking out of the hotel.

"Where are you taking me?" Jen squealed delightedly as the car veered around a sharp corner and headed down toward one of the most rundown areas in all of Burgundy. They passed a crumbling farmhouse on the right, then a smaller dwelling with a yardful of chickens, neglected fields and two rusting automobiles. Finally they stopped in front of what appeared to be a seedy beer parlor.

"The best coffee in Burgundy." Pierre hopped out of the car and ran around to open her door. "Just so you don't come away with the impression that everything in France is picture-book pretty. I guarantee you," he whispered as they entered the stale-smelling place, "the Dukes of Burgundy did not found Madame Orraine's."

"Bonjour, Madame!" Pierre greeted the decrepit white-haired woman with a low bow, taking her hand and kissing it. Then he presented Jenifer with the same polite flourish. It was as if he were presenting her to royalty.

"The usual, Madame." He nodded and led Jen to one of three rickety tables that were wedged in among a variety of electronic game machines.

"It's wonderful, isn't it?" Pierre gazed around the cobwebby bar with a fond smile. A fat yellow cat swirled around Jen's ankles, then hopped onto the table and rubbed against Pierre's face.

133

"De Gaulle." Pierre tickled the cat under its chin. "Nobody comes to Madame Orraine's who objects to pussycats on the table. Well, de Gaulle can scarcely be thought of as just a pussycat. As soon as Madame puts on the tablecloth he will be gone. He has the manners of a prince."

Jen shook her head in astonishment. That this formal, mysterious Pierre Rennes, owner of the elegant La Petite Auberge, could be smitten with a place as eccentric and bizarre as Madame Orraine's made him even more endearing.

Pierre leaned forward, whispering as de Gaulle continued to rub against his cheek, "Madame was in the French Resistance. She is one of the most decorated women in France."

Jen cast a quick look at the tiny white-haired lady whose erect bearing did in fact give her a queenly attitude.

"This de Gaulle is de Gaulle the sixth. The original de Gaulle was Madame's associate during the war years and he, too, was instrumental in overcoming the Nazis." Pierre plopped the pussycat down onto the floor as Madame spread a clean white cloth on the table and placed two steaming cups of thick black coffee in front of them. Moments later she returned with a loaf of crusty bread, a crock of soft cheese and a pot of deep-purple plum preserves. Then, much to Jen's surprise, she pulled up a chair and joined them.

Madame Orraine loved Americans. She wanted to know all about Duffy, Iowa. What kind of chickens were most popular, what kind of cows were they breeding for milk and what kind for beef? What did Jen think of Burgundy and in particular what did she think of the food at the Auberge? For the next hour Jen struggled to keep up with the

134

conversation and only once did Pierre come to her rescue. As they left, Madame Orraine nodded discreetly to Pierre and Jen blushed, knowing that she had received top honors from one of his most highly esteemed friends.

They were silent as they drove away from Madame Orraine's. No explanation was necessary. Jen understood perfectly why he cherished the old lady. It no longer struck her as odd or ironic that such a dignified woman with such an illustrious past would opt to run a slightly seedy coffeehouse filled with electronic games. Madame liked young people. She did not like the electronic games but used them, as she said, as a decoy, to lure young people into her establishment. According to Pierre, the young, rowdy youth inevitably abandoned the games for conversation with Madame Orraine. Although that morning they had been her only customers, Pierre said that from three in the afternoon till closing the place was jammed.

"What next?" Jen snuggled against him as they drove out into the countryside. The *vendanges* was in full swing and the vineyards were alive with the laughter of those employed to harvest the crop of grapes.

"You never told me why you're not slaving over your hot stove today?"

"I called early this morning." Pierre kissed the top of her head. "Michel is taking over during the lunch period. He seldom gets the opportunity and of course he likes nothing better than to be in charge without me barking at him constantly."

"You?" Jen feigned total disbelief. "You? Bark?"

"Rarely." Pierre grinned. "But on occasion I find it necessary in order to keep my volatile reputation afloat."

135

Jen nodded. She had never witnessed the famous Rennes temperament firsthand, although she had seen a glimpse of its potential last night when he spoke of Catherine and his reason for keeping her picture. A wave of uneasiness swept over her as she recalled his bitterness. According to class gossip the two had been separated for over three years. Shouldn't such bitterness have subsided by now?

Pierre pulled the car off the road, stopping by a stone wall that bordered a vast expanse of ripe grapes. In the distance the pickers were singing as they piled the old wooden wagons high with the succulent magenta bunches. The air was redolent of the heady scent of wine.

"This is my vineyard." Pierre gestured proudly. "My house is just beyond that hill."

"I didn't know you had a vineyard." Jen counted at least twenty people stooping over the thickly gnarled vines.

"A very minor vineyard." Pierre laughed. "Nothing like Meursault or even St. Romain. But it is a pleasant wine and makes a good modest offering at the Auberge. There is almost nothing I dislike more than an establishment that presents only an expensive selection of wines. It seems very snobbish and elitist to offer a customer only Lafites or Chambertins, Montrachets or Clos du Mouches."

"You've lost me." Jen shook her head.

"I'll never lose you." Pierre held her eyes for a moment. "At least I hope I won't."

He frowned suddenly as if an unpleasant thought had crossed his mind, then he started the motor. "I'd like to show you my estate."

"Pierre . . . I'm not sure . . . if someone sees us . . ."

"No one will be there," he interrupted, placing his hand lightly on her knee.

And no one was there. He led her into the centuries-old stone farmhouse and she was glad he did not feel the need to explain away the disarray, the partially reconstructed walls, the missing floorboards, the complete and utter chaos of the place he called home. Jen waded through the mess with an enchanted smile, as if she could already see, as he so obviously could, the finished product. He mentioned only that the renovation had been under way for nearly two years and that he had had difficulty finding high-caliber craftsmen to execute his ideas.

Of course he would want perfection. Jen followed him up the narrow staircase and into his sparsely furnished bedroom. The room was dominated by a giant four-poster bed replete with a tapestry and a blue and violet brocade canopy. Although the paint on the walls was peeling, the ceiling was cracked and the mullioned windows were taped closed, Jen was looking at the room through his eyes. She saw that it would be both majestic and touched with a simple warmth. When he held out his hand she was drawn willingly into his arms.

Behind the drawn curtains they made love, silently, slowly, with none of the furor that had possessed them the night before. They stared deeply and seriously into each other's eyes, savoring each delectable moment as if they each needed to make absolutely certain that no detail would escape unnoticed. They were so deeply in tune that

137

there was no need for words. It had been a perfect day, a blessing.

She must have dozed, because when she opened her eyes Pierre, wearing a loosely sashed maroon silk robe, was standing next to the bed, holding a silver tray.

"Breakfast in bed." He leaned over and kissed her as he placed the tray on the bed next to her. "A little late but . . . ? What is it you Americans say? It's the thought that counts."

Jen blinked and shifted down underneath the covers. "You shouldn't cook on your afternoon off. Pierre, really . . . you didn't need . . ."

"Taste . . ." He passed a plate to her with a somber expression.

"What?" Jen blinked harder as she took in his offering. It looked for all the world like a sandwich . . . a peanut-butter sandwich!

Before she could comment or even take a bite Pierre whisked a silver lid off one of the bowls, revealing a large bag of Tortilla Chips.

"Pierre!" Jen shrieked excitedly, and nearly tipped the tray over. "What is this?"

"What does it look like?" Pierre ripped open the bag of Doritos chips and plunged his hand inside.

"You said breakfast in bed . . . ?"

"Poetic license." Pierre popped a Doritos chip into her mouth.

"Oh, this is good!" Jen munched with an ecstatic smile. "How did you know I loved corn chips?"

"Everyone loves chips." Pierre winked and helped himself to another handful. "*And* Peanut butter and jelly sandwiches . . . everyone likes those, too."

"This is really peanut butter and jelly?" Jen picked up the sandwich with a reverential expression on her face. "How did you . . . where did you . . . ?"

"The imported food department down at Henri's market." He sat cross-legged at the foot of the bed and helped himself to a sandwich.

"Imported food?" Jen shook her head, laughing. "Peanut butter? Imported food? A delicacy? Well, I guess it depends on where you are. We import *foie gras* and truffles, you import peanut butter."

"I'd say it was a fair trade." Pierre laughed. "Though frankly, I think if I had to choose one of the three I'd choose the peanut butter."

"This from the famous Chef Rennes? Pierre, people would be horrified if they knew you were a junk-food addict!"

"I know." Pierre savored his sandwich with a peaceful expression.

"You really like it?" Jen was still flabbergasted.

"I love it." Pierre's dark eyes twinkled.

After two sandwiches each, one complete bag of corn chips and a quart of orange juice, they emerged laughing from Pierre's house and climbed back into the Citroën.

"I don't feel like cooking tonight," Pierre admitted as he dropped her off at a discreet distance from Madame Pauline's. "Why don't you come to the Auberge for dinner? Be my guest as I suggested. It would give me great pleasure to know I was cooking for you."

"Some other time," Jen promised.

"I don't want to leave you . . ." Pierre reached for her but she quickly opened the car door and got out.

"You know I want to see you tonight. . . ." He leaned across the seat.

"I know." Jen held his eyes a moment longer.

139

They had already agreed that two sleepless nights would be more than either of them could bear, so they would not see each other until Sunday evening.

"Go on," Jen scolded him lightly, "you'll be late and you'll have to make up for it by yelling at everyone!"

"I love you," he mouthed. "I'll see you Sunday evening!"

Jen walked back to Madame Pauline's with a tranquil smile on her face, climbed the stairs to her room and fell into bed wondering how Pierre was going to find the energy to get through the next twenty-four hours. Almost immediately she fell into a deep sleep. The next morning, after attending the early service at a nearby church, Jen pedaled out to the Auberge and spent the afternoon poring over cookbooks, trying to make up her mind what she would cook for her final class project. But her mind kept wandering . . . to Pierre, to her sons back in Duffy, to the fantasy restaurant she would one day open.

By the time she arrived at Madame Pauline's to dress for the evening she was pressed for time. At Pierre's request she had agreed to attend a wine tasting at the famed hospice in the center of Beaune. It was to be a gala affair and everyone in the class would be there. Since they had agreed to keep news of their romantic involvement secret, Pierre had convinced her that the best way to throw people off was for him to escort Jeannete and then meet Jen at the appointed corner twenty minutes after he left the hospice.

"Going to the tasting?" Albert called up to her as she descended the stairs around eight o'clock.

"Thinking about it." Jen ran her hand along the

140

banister and slowed her descent. In fact, she was already dressed to go. She was wearing the same slim black skirt and black sweater with the plunging neckline that she had worn that first night in Paris with Pierre. Only now, because of her weight loss, her curves were even more deliciously defined.

"You can't just think about it." Albert took her hand as she reached the bottom of the staircase. "Besides, you have your coat. Come, I'll walk over with you."

The moment she entered the crowded, smoke-filled room Jen knew it had been a mistake to come. She deplored the idea of seeing Pierre under pretenses like this. And even though he had made it clear that he and Jeannete were just friends, she hated seeing his arm linked through hers. Worst of all, she felt like a fraud making pleasant conversation with Albert as a way of dispelling any suspicions that might be aroused.

"Hello, you two!" Pierre joined Jen and Albert as they stood at the head of a lavishly appointed table.

Jen felt a tremor of excitement as Pierre's sleeve brushed against her bare arm. Her heart was fluttering like crazy and she could not bring herself to look directly at him. How could he be so relaxed and unruffled? She listened with a stiff smile pasted on her face as Pierre and Albert conversed in rapid French. She was so nervous she couldn't concentrate on English, let alone French. When Jeannete came to retrieve Pierre she was relieved.

"Let's try some wine," Albert suggested, leading her through the crowd to the tasting table. But even though Pierre was nowhere in sight she could not relax. Why had she allowed him to talk her into coming? She would have been happier just to have met him later. It was bad enough meeting him on the sly, but to risk giving herself away in front of Albert, or anyone else for that matter, was foolish. Several minutes later she sensed his presence next to her. She kept up a steady course of conversation with Albert. Nellie and Edgard had joined them and were chatting happily while Jen knew that Pierre's eyes were on her. Damn! Why did it seem as if he was enjoying this intrigue? His laughter kept interrupting her train of thought. She glanced at her watch. It was only eight-thirty. The plan was that he would leave at nine-thirty and she would meet him twenty minutes later. And what if someone followed her? Slip out quietly, he had said, without saying anything to anyone. No one will notice, there will be so many people there. Only they hadn't counted on Albert's escorting her to the party. And knowing Albert, he would feel entitled to see her home as well.

By nine o'clock Jen could stand the tension no longer. Brushing up against Pierre, she whispered, "I can't meet you. . . ." She prayed that no one noticed, feeling like a small-time Mata Hari. Pierre met her eyes briefly, nodded and turned back to the three gentlemen with whom he was talking.

Never again, she told herself as she located her coat and fled out into the night. She would never play that cloak and dagger game again.

But she would miss seeing him later. Abruptly, she stopped walking. Her body ached for him. She had looked forward to going back to his house, to the laughter and the peanut-butter sandwiches and . . .

Climbing the stairs in Madame Pauline's, she let

herself into her room and prepared for bed. In the future their plans to meet would have to be more carefully thought out. She slipped into bed but could only toss fitfully. She was worrying what he must be thinking about her decision not to meet him. Damn, it was too complicated. She willed herself to fall asleep but her heart leaped each time a car drove up out front, each time the door downstairs opened or the stairs creaked as the others came home.

By two in the morning she was still thrashing about. She toyed with the idea of phoning him but he had had so little sleep in the past two days she hated to do that. She would see him tomorrow in class. Wasn't that soon enough?

Somehow she fell asleep. The next morning she even managed to pull herself together to arrive at the Auberge an hour early. She headed straight for Pierre's office, expecting him to be bent over his desk as he usually was in the early morning hours.

"Monsieur Rennes has been called to Paris on business." Pierre's assistant, Michel, was seated behind Pierre's desk. "I am taking over the morning class."

Gone to Paris? On business? Pierre had said nothing about going to Paris. Something must have come up unexpectedly last night after he returned home from the hospice.

"Honey, what is it?" Nellie found her sitting in the herb garden after the morning session. "You look all strung out."

"Insomnia," Jen said, summoning a bright smile.

"You didn't drink enough of that good wine last night," Nellie laughed. "That would have put you to sleep sure."

"Maybe you're right," Jen admitted.

143

"Come with us to Gevrey-Chambertin this afternoon after the work session. We're going to pick grapes."

"Pick?" Jen perked up. "That sounds like fun."

"I'll meet you in an hour," Nellie promised.

Jen was ready when the knock came on her door. She burst out of the room in a pair of faded blue jeans and her oldest University of Iowa sweatshirt. Nellie commented on her change of spirits, and indeed Jen was feeling much happier. She had returned to her room to find a message waiting for her from Pierre. He was returning from Paris late in the afternoon and would meet her at their appointed corner after he finished work that night!

Almost until dusk Jen labored alongside Nellie and several other members of the class, picking the delicate red grapes that would become one of the richest red Burgundies made. By the time they trudged into the village from the vineyards, the streets were alive with music and dancing. Long tables were laden with cheese, bread and *vin ordinaire.*

"I've already had more wine than I've tasted in my entire life!" Jen was exhilarated from the experience. All afternoon they had sipped on a raw robust young wine, laughing and singing, mostly in French. This year's grape harvest was bountiful and the spirit which permeated the village was wild and joyous. In fact, never in her life had she witnessed such a sense of thanksgiving, boisterous and rowdy as it was.

"It is an excuse to celebrate life," Edgard laughed, his face flushed from so much wine.

"I'm turning into a Francophile," Nellie said, putting her arms around his neck. They danced off in a rollicking polka.

144

Jen abandoned herself to the celebratory feeling that permeated the town square, dancing with anyone who offered a hand—boys, old men, young men and, in the French style, several women. Back in Iowa she had, in her youth, been fond of square dancing, but this wild exchanging of partners, this twirling and stamping, surpassed everything she had ever known with its gusto.

And the wine never stopped flowing. When the music switched to contemporary rock tunes, Albert took her hand and together they caused a minor stir with their dancing.

"You know what they say." Edgard cut in on Albert when the music turned slower. "I forget the name of the place, I forget the name of the girl, but the wine . . . was Chambertin."

"Who said that?" Jen laughed.

"I believe it was Hilaire Belloc and it is true. Of course we are not drinking Chambertin here tonight, but still there is an essence of its flavor even in this raw wine. And it is in the air."

"I know what you mean." Jen followed Edgard to the sidelines, where Nellie was engrossed in conversation with two young women.

Jen accepted another glass of wine and danced with one of the men with whom she had picked grapes. If only Pierre could have been here to share such a joyous experience. But no, they had to hide. There would be no dancing in the square, no shared hilarity . . . Pierre! Jen shook her head, trying to clear it. The wine was finally having its effect, her head was reeling. It was after ten and she was supposed to meet Pierre at ten-thirty!

She finished the dance, then moved across the square to sit alone on the steps leading up to the old church. Her mind felt quite numb. If only she could put her head down on the steps for just a few minutes, everything would clear up inside her head.

"Jenifer . . . are you all right?" She looked up to see Albert leaning out of his car window. "Can I give you a ride back into Beaune?"

She stood up shakily and moved toward the car oblivious to everything except getting home and falling into her own bed.

"Why don't you stretch out on the backseat?" Albert suggested, guiding her into the car.

Jen protested. "I'm fine. Really."

"Just lie down." He smiled understandingly and for the first time Jen felt his concern was genuine. "I'll go tell Nellie and Edgard that I'm driving you."

The seat felt so good! Jen curled up gratefully.

"It happens sometimes, you know." Albert returned and she felt the car begin to move. "Just close your eyes. When you get home take two Alka-Seltzer and eat a piece of stale bread before you go to sleep. By tomorrow you'll feel fine."

"Thank you," Jen murmured. "Thank you, Albert."

The next thing she knew she was being lifted out of the backseat of the car. She draped her arm around his neck. "I've never done this . . ." she murmured, resting her head against him.

"Don't mention it."

She would go inside, follow Albert's suggestions and somehow find the strength to phone Pierre before she fell into bed. She should never have had so much wine. She should have known better. But maybe it was no accident. Maybe she had wanted to lose herself, to forget that her involvement with Pierre was leading nowhere.

146

"I can walk." She felt the fog begin to lift as Albert fumbled at the gate. Not until he had placed her down on her own two feet did she see Pierre's yellow Citroën pull to a stop.

He had seen. He had seen Albert carrying her up the walk! She felt Albert's hand on her waist drawing her inside the iron gate. At the same time Pierre was striding toward them, eyes blazing, hands clenched at his side.

"Monsieur . . ." Albert seemed momentarily shocked by Pierre's presence. "What brings you to Madame Pauline's?"

Jen held her breath. Pierre was drawing all the wrong conclusions, but surely he wouldn't ruin everything by venting his anger on her now.

"Madame Pauline and I are old friends," Pierre replied in a less than civil tone, his eyes never leaving Jen's face. "I often stop by for a drink after work."

"Of course." Albert nodded but Jen recognized the snide tone in his voice. If he had suspected before that something existed between Jen and Pierre, Pierre's anger had confirmed it.

CHAPTER NINE

Oh, how stupid she had been! The next morning Jen awoke with a ferocious hangover, furious with herself for having had so much to drink. Not only did she feel wretched, but now Pierre was mad at her as well. And rightly so. Yes, the entire mess was all her own doing.

She dragged herself into the bathroom and stood under a cool shower. You could take the girl out of Iowa but apparently you could not take Iowa out of the girl. She just wasn't accustomed to such a complicated life. And now, no doubt Albert was scheming away, fueled by Pierre's appearance at Madame Pauline's.

After dressing, Jen sat on the edge of her bed watching the hands of her travel clock creep toward the hour when she would have to see Pierre in class. Her head ached. She was too miserable even to cry. Damn! How had she been so stupid, so careless! It wasn't like her at all.

She could not bring herself to go downstairs for

a cup of coffee and on impulse knocked on Nellie's door.

"Oh . . . lovey!" Nellie drew Jen inside her room and poured her a cup of tea, which she brewed every morning with her electric teakettle.

"You know?" Jen gave her a stark hopeless look.

Nellie nodded. "I know Monsieur Rennes was here to see you, that he made some silly assumption about Albert and . . ."

"I've behaved like a fool." Jen looked away bleakly. "Like a child."

"You didn't do a thing!" Nellie exclaimed. "You had a wonderful time and drank too much wine—though not so much, I should imagine, as Edgard, who is so out of it that we shall be lucky to see him by tomorrow evening."

Jen gave Nellie a dubious look.

"Seriously, Jen"—Nellie plopped down on the bed and faced her squarely—"please talk to me about it. You can trust me."

"I know I can." Jen felt the tears rise in her throat. All these weeks she had kept everything to herself. Now it appeared that she and Pierre had been totally unsuccessful at hiding their feelings for each other.

"Nellie, I . . . oh, it's so complicated."

"Maybe it's not as complicated as you think. Jen, I've thought for some time that Monsieur Rennes had a soft spot for you."

"It's gone further than that," Jen confessed, and then she went back to the beginning, back to the chance meeting in Paris, to their mutual decision not to see each other and finally to the second chance encounter in Meursault.

Nellie listened attentively with a soft smile on her round face. "You haven't said if you love him."

Jen swallowed back her tears. Of course she loved him! She loved him so much she'd tried to forget by drinking all that wine. Tried to forget how it was going to feel leaving him.

"Look, Jen, he's a wonderful man. I've seen the way he looks at you. I've never believed those malicious rumors about him . . . about all the women in his life, about his tempestuous relationship with Catherine. That's 'man talk.' . . . No, it's true, Jenny. All that bitchy gossip about Pierre is some sort of misplaced envy. You and I know what sort of a man he is. We're women. We sense how good he is."

"Oh, Nellie . . ." Jen turned against the side of the chair and sobbed. It felt good to cry, good to let it all out.

After a minute she composed herself and looked back at Nellie. "It's just that I'm afraid I've blown everything. Albert can be mean, we both know that, he could make this last week and a half really miserable for me. And now Pierre thinks . . . Probably he'll take his anger out on me, too. Maybe he won't even give me the certificate."

"Nonsense!" Nellie interrupted forcefully. "Pierre Rennes has more integrity than that and you know it. You're allowing your imagination to run away with you. Jen, you're being too hard on yourself. You had too much to drink. You were tired, confused, worried about your future with Pierre. Now I understand what's been going on with you these past few weeks. Good heavens, Jenifer, you've been cloistering yourself away night after night, trying to shut off your emotions. Then when you and Pierre finally get together you're besieged with even more worries. Go easy on yourself, girl."

"I thought I was having a good time at the *vendanges*. I thought . . ."

". . . and so you were!" Nellie interjected brightly. "You just overdid it. It would all have turned out differently if I'd been able to drag Edgard away and you'd arrived back here with us the way you left. Just go to Pierre and explain."

But Jenifer was in no way prepared for Pierre's reaction. Throughout the morning class and again in the afternoon session he was every bit the tyrant he was reputed to be, barking at Albert, at Nellie, insulting Jen's clumsiness at deboning a chicken.

Talk to him? Jen thought as she biked back to the village later. Nellie had made it sound so simple this morning. Suddenly Jen jumped off her bike, turned around and rode straight back to the Auberge, where she headed for Pierre's private office. She braced herself as she knocked on his door. She would make it brief because he would soon be in the kitchen preparing for the evening.

"I'm busy," he growled loudly in French.

Jen drew in a deep breath and knocked again. There was a moment's silence, and then the door swung open. Pierre stood aside for her to enter, shooting her a critical glance.

"I'm sorry about last night." She faced him as he closed the door. "I went over to Gevrey-Chambertin with Nellie and Edgard. We spent the afternoon picking grapes for Monsieur du Pres and went on to the celebration in town. I drank way too much and Albert kindly offered me a ride home. That was all there was to that. As to my not phoning you to say I wouldn't be meeting you . . . that's another matter."

151

"It didn't occur to you that I might be worried about you?" Pierre flared.

Jen shook her head. "By the time I realized how late it was I . . . I couldn't think clearly."

"I've got to hand it to you"—Pierre whipped off his necktie in an angry gesture—"you had me fooled."

"What do you mean?" Jen stiffened.

"I wouldn't have thought you capable of it." He shot her a wounding glance.

"Just say it, Pierre," Jen told him.

"I say . . . I say you've been using me in this little romantic adventure. Look, I know how competitive these classes are. You think I don't know how much it means to come in first? All the publicity? The gold seal and so forth . . ."

"How could you think that?" Jen was on the verge of tears. "Pierre . . ." She reached out to touch his arm but he pulled away. "Pierre, I'm so sorry . . . I don't know how you could think . . ." She broke off abruptly. Why on earth was she apologizing for his insult to *her?*

"Stop apologizing!" He turned on her vehemently. "At least take responsibility for your motives and stop resorting to tears."

"I'm not resorting to tears!" Jen faced him defiantly, undaunted by his anger, aware that her own outrage was quite equal to his.

"You are!" he countered. "You are slipping into the role of victim. Oh, I know how that's done. I have seen how women can twist the truth, end up by crying so I'm the one who feels like an ogre. Don't play the victim with me or I'll walk out this minute. If you face me with the truth, you can still salvage something from this nasty business."

"I came here to apologize, to explain"—Jen

marched around to face him—"and that is not playing the victim! All right, yes, I started to cry. But not to get your sympathy. Out of frustration . . . yes, I started to cry out of frustration."

"This is a bad time." Pierre's mouth was strained and tense. "Really, you couldn't have chosen a worse time to have this discussion. . . . Something has come up. I have to go to Paris on business again. More nasty business."

"Paris? Again? When are you leaving?" Jen felt her sense of panic heighten.

"I've no idea." Pierre opened his top desk drawer and slammed it shut. "I've got several large parties booked this week, the schedule here is in shambles. I don't know how I'll fit it in . . . probably drive up after work . . ."

"If I could help . . ." Jen had to stop herself from reaching out to him. He looked so miserable.

"No." He did not even look at her but sat back down at his desk and began writing.

So, he was turning her off. Inadvertently she caught sight of another picture of Catherine Rennes looking haughtily out of its silver frame on the corner of his desk. Unable to control her sense of outrage, she thrust it angrily into his face.

"There is something perverse about keeping this around! You want to keep all that bitterness alive. That's why it's here. And that's why you refuse to listen to what I'm saying to you now."

"Jenifer, I know that you slept with me to gain . . ."

"You don't believe that!" Jen shouted. "You're using that as an excuse."

"I'd respect you more"—he took a step toward her—"if you'd just admit it."

"I'd respect you more if you'd either admit

153

you're still in love with your ex-wife or toss this thing out!"

They stared at each other, rigidly, their bodies taut with anger. Finally Jen spoke in a low, controlled voice. "You know I don't give a damn about Albert. You know that!"

She turned away and walked toward the door. "The reason I had too much to drink last night, though I didn't realize it at the time, was to try and forget about how much I love you, because I don't know how I'm going to live the rest of my life without you."

She was already reaching for the doorknob when she felt his hand on her shoulder. He turned her around slowly. His dark eyes were moist and he looked at her a long time before speaking.

"I apologize for what I said."

Jen reached up and touched his chin tenderly. "Me, too."

"I do love you." Pierre gazed at her earnestly. "I'm glad you burst in here. This business in Paris has me . . ." He broke off with a wave of his hand. "Has me . . . I'm not myself. Please believe how deeply I love you."

Jen nodded tearfully. She believed him. She really did believe him.

"I thought I would go crazy when I saw you in Albert's arms . . ." Pierre took her in his arms and his mouth covered hers in a long, pleading kiss. He held her urgently, then suddenly pulled away. "I knew it was an irrational reaction. You'd told me you had no use for Jamin, but I . . ."

"It's all right." Jen drew his mouth back down on hers, nipping tenderly at his warm, full lips until he parted them.

His hands found her breasts and as they kissed

154

he stroked the fuzzy lavender sweater until her nipples swelled and hardened in eagerness. He teased her trembling breasts and she pressed against him, remembering how he, too, had responded to her touch.

Pierre removed one hand from her breast and pressed more tightly against her as he reached over her shoulder. She heard a door bolt slip into place. An erotic contraction seized her with the knowledge that he had bolted the door and her body responded, thrusting fervently against him. She felt his powerful arousal in answer to her pliant curves and the gentle rocking motion she instinctively initiated.

Her mind was far off. Only Pierre existed, only his hard muscular back under her hand, only his demanding mouth on hers, his hands spread fanlike on her hips, molding her seductively into him.

They sank onto the carpeted floor as one, their lips clinging hungrily together, their hands urgently stroking. Kneeling there, face to face, they pulled apart to stare at each other, their bodies tensed as if they might explode at any moment. Pierre swept the lavender sweater over her head and tossed it aside. His eyes never left her face as he unfastened her bra and lifted it gently forward off her shoulders.

The roman shades were lowered and the small oak-paneled office was suffused with the soft late afternoon light. She watched in a state of heightened eroticism as Pierre stripped naked and stretched out on his side, pulling her down to face him. He buried his dark head between her full breasts and she shuddered at the delicious tingling he evoked. She caressed his pale flanks audaciously, driven by his deft tongue circling against her nipple.

"It's going to be all right," he crooned as his hand slid up her leg and he tugged at her panty hose. "It really is." He drew the sheer stockings below her knees and began stroking her thighs, warming her, infusing her with a desire so fierce that she caught his hair in her hands and arched forward. The provocative prodding of his fingers unleashed a tangle of breathtaking convulsions. Her heart accelerated as his fingers swam against her, propelling her closer and closer to the agonizing brink of ecstasy, then pulling back. She was writhing against him, beside herself at the power of the sensuous, fiery feelings emanating from his touch.

"It's going to be all right." His reassurance rang inside her head and she caressed him. It seemed as if he were speaking to himself as well as to her.

"I know, I know it is," she gasped, arching her neck back, clenching her teeth to contain the unbearable pleasure unleashed by the full weight of his formidable body covering hers.

Now they rocked as one, in complete abandon, as if by coming together they were finally free. The perfection of their bodies moving in frantic unison fed them both. Desire swelled with each sharp movement, each searing connection of hot, quivering flesh. They twisted and rolled, oblivious of everything but their mutual ecstasy and the soft hushed shadows which seemed to mute their ragged breathing.

Time passed and did not pass. What seemed to have been an eternity of passionate abandon reached its shattering climax swiftly and they lay panting in each other's arms.

Pierre's heart seemed to be pounding inside Jen's head. She shifted slightly, looking up at him, aware for the first time of the predinner hum outside the office.

Pierre's cheeks were crimson, his dark hair damp on his forehead. He looked like a roguish boy caught in a compromising position. Suddenly they collapsed against each other, laughing breathlessly like naughty children.

"I swear to you"—Pierre brushed her tangled hair back away from her face—"*that* was the furthest thing from my mind."

"It was from mine, too," Jen admitted.

She resisted the urge to scramble around for her clothes. It had all happened so fast, like a violent tornado whipping through and leveling everything in sight. She had had no resistance, neither in her mind nor her body.

"Do you know, I just had that new bolt put on the door." Pierre located her bra and offered it to her. "I got tired of people barging in here while I'm trying to work. I swear, I just had the thing installed yesterday!"

"Timing is everything," Jen quipped as she pulled her panty hose back up and smoothed out her skirt.

Pierre continued chuckling and shaking his head as he pulled on his white chef's trousers and slipped on his white coat. "Were we having a fight?"

"No." Jen pulled on her sweater and stood up. "We were making up. That's how it's done."

"I like it." Pierre looked at her gently. "I've never known much about making up. Thank you for teaching me."

157

Before the kiss could develop there was a loud knock at the door.

"How many of those do you suppose we didn't hear?" Jen whispered with a grin. For the moment what anyone thought was the furthest thing from her mind. As Pierre went to the door she turned away, straightening her sweater and running her hands through her hair to give some semblance of propriety.

"Well, hello." She turned to see Eric Martin staring at them with his most obsequious smile.

"What is it, Eric?" Pierre's tone was polite but clipped.

"I thought we had an appointment." Eric addressed Pierre solemnly, and then checked his watch as if to make sure.

"I don't recall one." Pierre crossed back to his desk and as he did Eric caught Jen's eye in an unmistakably malevolent look. "No, I don't see it here, Eric."

"*Pardon, si'l vous plaît.*" Eric shook his head in a display of impatience with himself. "I don't know what's wrong with me lately. I'm either an hour early or a day late. Please forgive the intrusion."

"That's all right." Pierre smiled and closed the door.

"Now, then." He gave Jen a come-hither glance. "What's the matter?"

"Do you think he heard us . . . ?"

"*Ma chère,* we were as quiet as mice, I assure you. Don't worry. These walls are very thick."

Jen shook her head worriedly. "Pierre, I'm not even concerned anymore about 'being found out' . . . I just think Eric is a bit off balance."

"Promise me not to worry." Pierre gathered up some papers on his desk and reached for her hand.

"Unfortunately my kitchen awaits me. Did you mean that about not caring who knows?"

"More or less." Jen smiled, trying to shake the apprehension aroused by Eric's intrusion.

"I love you." Pierre escorted her to the door. "I'll tell you what would make me happy. Sharing my kitchen with you."

"Not on your life!" Jen felt giddy at the suggestion. "Share your kitchen?" she teased as they went outside. "You could never share your kitchen with anyone, Pierre. I'd be taking my life in my hands. After all, your kitchen is your kingdom."

"Well"—Pierre pressed his lips together in an ambiguous half-smile—"maybe not really *share* my kitchen."

Jen met his eyes laughing and turned to run back to where she had parked her bike.

For the next four days Pierre's comment about sharing his kitchen reverberated happily inside her head. Even though he picked her up at their appointed corner every night after work and they slept together in his curtained bed, the remark was the one tangible reference he had made to the possibility of a future together. And for the moment it was enough. The bliss of spending her nights with Pierre plus the excitement and last-minute acceleration of activity as the course drew to an end were more than enough to occupy Jen's mind.

There wasn't even time to think about going home. Though she wrote the boys daily, most of her free time was spent perfecting her chosen recipes in the test kitchen.

"I wanted to do a 'sort of' Wellington." Nellie was grousing late Friday afternoon. She and Jen were the only ones remaining in the test kitchen and as usual Nellie was having trouble with her Waterloo, puff pastry.

"Yours is always perfect." Nellie threw Jen a wicked look, then laughed. "Tell me I've made a poor choice, Jen. Tell me to abandon my idea of pulling off this sort of Nellie Wellington *à la* Rennes and be satisfied with something less spectacular. I'm not going to come in first anyway, so what's the point."

Jen dabbed her finger in one of the three bowls of sauce she was testing, tasted and added a pinch of mint and a tablespoon of heavy cream. The second bowl received only the heavy cream, and the third, mint and a teaspoon of vinegar. Following her instincts again, she had decided to prepare a basically simple menu for the final competition, which would be judged the following Friday, not only by Pierre and one other three-star French chef, but also by two Michelin representatives, a well-known Italian chef and the author of one of the most definitive books on Chinese cuisine.

"Did you hear me?" Nellie cast Jen an envious look, marveling at her concentration as she slaved over the sauce for the extra-thick lamb chops, her choice for the entrée.

"I think I've got it!" Jen jotted down a measurement in her notebook, took another taste from the third bowl and turned her full attention to Nellie. "You should stick with the Wellington, Nel. I disagree with Edgard. That's what you want to cook and that's what you should cook. Your way."

"But what about my puff pastry?" Nellie lamented, looking at the buttery mass in front of her.

"Do it faster," Jen advised. "You think you're going to foul it up so you're extra meticulous. Just do it by feel. Really! Do a test. Measure out three sets of ingredients."

"Expensive . . ." Nellie shuddered.

"I know." Jen grinned. "Measure them out ahead and then just do them each, quick. I'll time you and I'll bet you a bottle of . . . let me not get too carried away here"—she laughed—"a bottle of Fleurie that the fastest will be the best."

"A very unorthodox approach," Nellie giggled. "I like it. Aren't you nervous about actually doing it? Oh, by the way, Edgard said he overheard Eric talking about a veal dish with Szechuan pepper, hazelnuts, tangerines and . . . you won't believe . . . olives! He must be out to please the Italian, the Chinese, the French . . . everyone in one dish. Why do you suppose the tangerines, though?"

Jen stood at the sink, rinsing off her dishes. "You know Eric is almost irrationally ambitious. I think he's capable of doing something very spiteful."

"Agatha Christie visits La Petite Auberge. You think he might slip something fatal into the *soupe du jour?*"

"I'm serious," Jen interrupted. "He not only dislikes Pierre, he's terribly envious, jealous. He's not interested in learning how to cook. We all knew that after the first week."

"Darling, I think your midwestern imagination is running rampant once again. This is *haute cuisine*, not cloak and dagger."

"Maybe." Jen dropped the subject. But later that afternoon as she shopped for a new dress to wear to the final banquet her thoughts returned to Pierre. Initially she had been relieved that he had decided to leave for Paris after work on Saturday. His absence would leave her free to practice her preparations and gird herself mentally for the competition. But as she thought of it now, she remembered the note of anxiety in his voice, and she wondered again what his business in Paris was, and why he would not discuss it with her.

She picked up a loosely knit black sweater with a low scoop neckline and stared at it, still thinking about Pierre and how much his well-being and happiness had come to mean to her. He took so much pride in La Petite Auberge, in the consistent excellence of his cuisine and in the way he led his life. Over the past week she had come to see that his bitterness over his marriage was not so much because of love lost but because he had failed, failed to marry the right woman. She knew now that Pierre Rennes could not abide failure.

She moved over to a full-length mirror and held up the sweater. She could wear it with her black skirt, add a new belt and save the expense of buying a new outfit.

Jen handed the sweater back to the saleswoman and left the boutique. Feeling quite preoccupied with all her thoughts, she considered riding back out to the test kitchen to work out the kinks in her chosen dessert. But somehow she found herself having a cup of coffee in Maxine's instead. She was joined minutes later by Eric Martin, who chatted amiably about how eager he was to return to Chicago and put his recently acquired knowledge to use. He made no mention of their calamitous evening in Meursault, of his unexpected declaration of love or of his intrusion into Pierre's office. When they left the café he gave her a chaste kiss on the cheek and waved her off as if they were the best of friends. He was, Jen thought as she climbed onto her bike, almost too nice.

CHAPTER TEN

Pierre left for Paris on Saturday, and for Jen the weekend dragged on interminably. Then on Sunday, just as Jen was feeling all tingly about seeing him in another few hours, Pierre phoned from Paris to say that a problem forced him to stay over and drive back on Monday. Monday night there was a special banquet booked at the Auberge, so the only opportunity they would have to see each other would be in class.

Still, with little more than a week remaining before she was due to fly black to the States, Jen managed to be optimistic. Since their mutual explosions in Pierre's office a new closeness had developed. There was a sense of connection that existed even when they weren't together. The tensions that dominated the early weeks were absent. Though they made it a point not to be seen together, not to exchange loving looks or indulge in other forms of intimate expression, the pressure of "being found out," as Pierre laughingly put it, was no longer a problem. They lived in the moment, leaving talk of the future for another time.

On Tuesday evening Pierre appeared at Madame Pauline's to pick Jen up.

"First we make love," Pierre whispered once she was seated beside him in the Citroën. "It has been too, too long."

"You're stopping?" Jen gave him a quizzical smile when he halted the car just around the corner.

"To kiss you." He drew her close in a deep, hungry kiss. "How I've missed you," he murmured. "And now"—he shifted the car into gear—"to my house for an appetizer. Then we are driving to Lyon as planned to dine at my friend Alain's bistro."

An hour later she lay in his arms, smiling and satisfied as she always was after they made love. Whatever had been troubling Pierre about the business in Paris had been remedied. His furrowed brow was relaxed and the edginess she had detected when he had first picked her up was gone.

"I wouldn't mind peanut-butter sandwiches." Jen snuggled against his broad chest. "You make the best peanut-butter sandwiches."

"It's cook's night out." Pierre patted her bare behind as he rolled off the disheveled bed. "Besides, I want you to meet Alain and see his place. It is very small, very charming. Very much, I should think, like the place you envision opening in Duffy."

Jen shivered at the thought of her return to Iowa, trying not to dwell on it. The drive south to Lyon, followed by a leisurely meal in front of a roaring fire at Alain's, was a success. The bistro was lovely, just as Pierre had promised.

As Tuesday was the only night the Auberge was closed, Jen had assumed they would return to his house after dinner. But by the time they reached the Beaune city limits she noted the tension she had sensed in him since his return from Paris had returned. When he pulled up in front of Madame Pauline's instead of taking her back to his house, she felt a flicker of uneasiness.

He did not want to talk about what had happened in Paris and she was certain that that was what was on his mind. As a matter of fact, since his return she had been walking on eggs to avoid any reference to the trip. Now that she thought of it, even his joviality at Alain's had been a bit excessive, as if he were trying to convince himself as well as her that nothing was bothering him.

"What's the matter?" She turned to him abruptly in the darkness of the car.

"Nothing." He switched off the ignition and leaned forward to kiss her.

"No!" Jen felt a sharp pang. "There *is* something the matter, Pierre. What happened in Paris? Something's different. . . . You've tried very hard all evening to pretend that nothing is on your mind . . ."

"Well, of course something is on my mind." He tried to make light of her observation.

"You're very good at keeping things to yourself." Jen took his hand and squeezed it. "If nothing is the matter, then why are you returning me to Madame's instead of to your bed?"

"I love you . . ." He drew her close in a long, searching kiss but she would not be dissuaded. She pulled away, looking at him closely.

"Can't you tell me?" she asked anxiously after a moment.

Pierre shook his head stiffly. "It is strictly business, Jenifer. Believe me. That's all I want to say at the moment."

Jen felt a stab of regret that he could not confide in her.

"You know I love you," he repeated softly, and she smiled. But the nagging sense of insecurity remained. Something had happened in Paris and he wasn't telling her.

The next day was Wednesday, and with only two more days before the final competition on Friday night there was a buzz of excitement at Madame Pauline's. All of the participants were on a strict budget and each was responsible for shopping for food items, since Pierre had from the outset stressed that fresh produce and high-quality ingredients were the mainstay of excellence. The idea of the competition was to see, all things being equal, who could create the finest culinary experience.

"Well, you were right about the puff pastry," Nellie said as she and Jen biked to the Auberge in a misty rain for the afternoon session.

"You've mastered your Waterloo, have you?" Jen glanced at the rosy-cheeked Englishwoman.

"I'm a nervous wreck about it," Nellie admitted. "I spent all morning alone in the test kitchen wrestling my dough into submission. I'm going to do it anyway. What the hell, right? If I win, I'll call my restaurant Duke Nellie's Wellington. Everyone is into trendy cute little names for their restaurants these days."

"Duke Nellie," Jen laughed. "I like it."

As they reached the top of the steep incline that

led to La Petite Auberge, Jen felt a quiver of excitement at the sight of a long black limousine parked in front.

"Do you suppose the Michelin judges have arrived early?" she asked Nellie as they wheeled their bikes around behind the test kitchen.

"Couldn't be the judges." Nellie craned her neck to stare at the impressive-looking vehicle. "They travel incognito, I think. They don't exactly sail around the countryside in that kind of *style.*"

Jen giggled nervously. "The Michelin judges." She pretended to quake with fear. "I always imagined them in long black judicial robes with great hooked noses and fleshy jowls, the guardians of France's most potent product . . . cuisine!"

"It's true," Nellie chuckled. "Everyone in the restaurant business in France lives in dread of their dictums. You know, there was a famous chef in Paris who jumped out of a window because Michelin took away one of his three stars. Fortunately, I believe he only sprained both ankles and got off with a few cuts. He was on the second floor."

"You made that up!" Jen laughed as they entered the classroom. Far from being the usual paragon of order and concentration, the room was buzzing with activity and speculation.

"She's here!" Albert rushed toward them with an excited glint in his eye.

"Who?" Nellie brushed by him, her eyes fastened on Edgard. He had remained apart from the flurry of activity with a downcast expression.

"Catherine Rennes!" someone announced.

Jen felt all the gaiety of the moment before, all of her enthusiasm, optimism and confidence, drain out of her at the sound of that name.

"She arrived just after noon!" Albert explained. "She *and* Monsieur Rennes, I should say. They arrived together in *her* car. Apparently the business trip Monsieur Rennes made to Paris netted him a little pleasure on the side. They were seen dining at Lasserre and now she's followed him here. I would say a reconciliation is in the offing!"

"I saw her!" another classmate enthused, his face glowing. "She is even more beautiful than her pictures. Absolutely breathtaking. She stepped out of her car as the chauffeur opened her door. She's not nearly as tall as she appears on screen, she's very tiny in fact, and she was pale, wearing not a speck of makeup, and yet she was so beautiful . . ." He broke off with an extravagant gesture.

"Nobody knows why she is here," Edgard spoke up and Jen knew his words were for her benefit. She moved to one of the refrigerators on the pretext of checking the consistency of her apricot mousse.

"Well, I can only add," Eric's voice rang in Jen's ears, "that I happened to drive by Monsieur's estate *very* late last night and her car was parked alongside his Citroën. If it isn't a reconciliation, let's at least hope they're having fun."

Jen clenched her fists and felt the color rise to her cheeks. Catherine had been waiting for him last night after he dropped her off at Madame Pauline's? Was that possible? Could he have known? Could he have kept it from her?

"Don't listen to all that." Nellie drew her aside. "She's his *ex*-wife. There could be any number of legitimate explanations for her appearance here. Those men out there are acting like a pack of drooling, idiotic adolescents. . . . Jen, darling . . . you mustn't let this throw you."

Jen forced a smile and went back to the apricot mousse. No, she would not let herself be thrown by this. But she was not going to be a fool any longer, either. She was going to be strictly realistic. She had been stupid to believe Pierre kept Catherine's picture everywhere for any other reason than that he still loved her. Perhaps he had wanted to believe he despised Catherine. Perhaps his growing feelings for Jen had driven him to see Catherine once more, to test his emotions. And when he'd seen Catherine, he realized he was still in love with her.

Jen's throat constricted in terror as she heard the door open. How could she stay? How could she face him?

Jen heard an unmistakable flicker of apprehension in Pierre's voice as he addressed the class. She looked at him evenly, betraying none of the hurt and bewilderment she had experienced moments before. He must not know what she was feeling.

Perhaps he thought word·of Catherine's arrival had not yet reached her. Yes, she was sure of it. As the class continued, Pierre relaxed. Jen's composure must have reassured him. Of course he would explain later. He wasn't cruel, she would never think that of him.

As the class drew to a close, Jen seized a moment to slip out the door when Pierre was busy explaining a detail to another student. She raced for her bike. For the moment, at least, her sense of accomplishment outweighed everything else—she had made it through the class.

Her escape was interrupted, however, when she spotted a slight blond figure leaning against the

169

side of the building. She caught her breath. It was her! Just then, Catherine Rennes stamped out the cigarette she had been smoking and turned around. Jen found herself face to face with the renowned beauty.

But the woman facing Jen possessed none of the sophistication or haughtiness she projected on film and in her pictures. The woman facing Jen had a fragile, ghostlike beauty . . . the face of a lost child with wide, questioning eyes and a pouty mouth. Far from the femme fatale, Catherine Rennes looked like a young girl.

She was beautiful. Jen climbed onto her bike and pedaled off. Yes, she was beautiful, disturbingly so, and in a way that Jen had not counted on. She was not some artificial made-up mask of a woman. She possessed a natural, haunting beauty.

How stupid! Jen pedaled furiously. How stupid she had been to think that she would be anything but a passing fancy to a man like Pierre.

By the time she reached Madame Pauline's she could feel herself crumbling. There was a message from Pierre to phone his office the minute she returned. She ignored it.

The inevitable had happened. Deep down, hadn't she known that it would? She pulled her suitcases out from under her bed and began to pack. She didn't plan to leave early, she would not try to run off. But she needed to keep busy, needed to keep moving. She rinsed out a few articles of clothes, dusted, built a fire, showered and dressed for the final dinner she had agreed to have with Nellie, Edgard and several other members of the class. Claudine, the maid, knocked on her door three times to tell her she had a phone call but Jen replied that she was busy and finally put out the

"Do Not Disturb" sign. Let him think what he wanted. A message was thrust under her door saying it was urgent that she phone Monsieur Rennes. Jen crumpled the paper and tossed it aside as if it were a meaningless scrap. There would be no scenes, no blame. She would leave with her dignity intact if it was the last thing she did.

She went downstairs and phoned home. The sound of her sons' voices was a balm to her wounded spirit. They were real, they were her life and she would be returning to them with so much more than she'd had when she left. In many ways she was a new woman. She had a confidence about herself, about her mind and her body that she had never felt before. No one could take that away. And she had a sense of purpose now, a clear vision of what the future might hold. Over the past weeks her idea of opening a catering business that would lead to running her own restaurant had taken on a concrete reality. Before she had been a dreamer. Now she knew she was a doer. She had not failed at all and she would not torment herself with such negativism. She had accomplished what she had come to France to do!

Back in her room, she sat stiffly in a chair, going over the details of her approaching flight until Nellie knocked on her door at nine-thirty.

"Did you talk to him?"

Jen shook her head as she slipped on a jacket.

"Well, he called didn't he?" Nellie demanded.

"I don't want to talk to—"

"You've *got to!*" Nellie grasped her shoulders. "Darling, you can't not talk to him! There's an explanation. Look at you! You're wound tight as a done-in watch spring. You can't last through the competition keeping everything so neatly under

171

control. You've got to at least get angry . . . if you've reason to. You don't mean to ignore him for the duration? Jen, that isn't like you."

"Nel . . . I know you want to help. Please . . . I can't talk . . . Maybe I shouldn't go to dinner."

"No, no!" Nellie backed off. "I'll leave off trying to offer my two cents. You've got to come with us! We're going to bang our beers on the table and act like bloody adolescent fools. That is probably the best thing you could do!"

Jen found it did help to sit in the midst of the rowdy group in the bistro, surrounded by the talk and commotion. Nellie was right. She couldn't stay wound this tight for the next two days. But neither could she entertain the idea of facing Pierre under anything but professional circumstances. What she needed was the distraction of the high-spirited exchange with the others.

After several beers the pain lodged in the pit of her stomach did not seem so important. She even laughed and told anecdotes about her sons, which made her feel warm, confident and even strangely hopeful. The evening was almost pleasant until around eleven-thirty, when she looked up to see Pierre and Catherine in the doorway of the bistro. They were shown to a secluded corner . . . a corner she would have to pass on her way out of Maxine's.

Jen glanced around the table. None of the others had seen them enter and that was some help. Perhaps she could make her exit without feeling everyone's scrutiny, without feeling Nellie's concern for her. She needed to get out . . . and fast!

"Don't go!" Edgard begged. "One more round!"

But she was convincing, and though her heart was pounding, she managed to laugh. She fortified herself with a sip of Edgard's beer and walked quickly through the smoke-filled bistro. She tried not to look at Catherine and Pierre, who sat hunched over their brandies, talking.

"Jenifer . . . !" Pierre's voice cut through her like a knife. For an instant she felt stunned. Leaping from his table, he took her hand and she found herself standing next to Catherine Rennes.

How could he be so insensitive? Jen wondered, acknowledging the introduction to Catherine, unaware that Pierre was still clutching her hand. She spoke to Catherine in French automatically, as if she were a figure in a dream.

"I'll phone you," Pierre told her quickly in English. For an instant Jen was aware of a wistful expression on Catherine Rennes's face.

Once outside, Jen struggled against the uncharacteristic impulse to barge back inside and confront him head on about his insensitivity in forcing her to meet his ex-wife. Now she was angry, angrier than she had ever been in her entire life. So angry that she was frightened by the violent impulses that welled up inside her. She ran all the way back to Madame Pauline's, one minute thinking she would stick it out to the end, the next moment determined to leave immediately for Paris and fly home the next day. No sense in trying to compete in the final cook-off when she felt like poisoning the master chef!

The phone was ringing as she entered and she answered it angrily, without thinking.

"I'm on my way over . . ." It was Pierre.

"No!" Jen slammed down the receiver and started off to her room. But she stopped midway on the stairs and turned back. She knew sleep would be impossible, so she ran outside and hopped on her bike. She would ride all night if necessary. She would ride and ride until the anger was used up.

Jen pedaled hard until she was gasping, but the anger would not subside. How could she have been so wrong about someone? Was there any way of perceiving herself as less than an imbecile in the whole affair? Imagine believing his stories about Catherine's pictures! That was the worst of it, that she had been so damned gullible! She could kill him . . . yes, the thought terrified her but there it was. She who could forgive anyone anything, who bent over backward to understand, felt for the moment that the only remedy for her fury and her pain would be knowing there was no more Pierre Rennes!

Suddenly she was crying. She gripped the handlebars as if her life depended on the contact with their hard, cold reality. No amount of anger could eradicate the love she felt for him. How was it possible? How was it possible to love someone and hate them with such violence?

Finally she stopped crying. She pedaled more slowly. By the time she pulled up in front of Madame Pauline's she was drained. She parked her bike around back and was about to go inside when she felt a presence in the shadows behind her.

"Go away," she said without turning.

"No." Pierre took her hand and turned her around. "I love you . . ."

His arms gripped her, pulling her close. He pressed her to him urgently. For an instant her body felt lifeless. Then his lips crushed down upon her, and she exploded into life.

"You had no business following me here!" she cried, pulling away from him, her anger rekindled

174

by the heat he had aroused. "You had no right to be waiting here for me!"

"You wouldn't answer my phone calls!" Pierre's dark eyes were angry.

"How dare you be angry!" Jen's temper flared. "How can *you* reproach me? Don't turn the tables around here. I didn't do a thing!"

"You refused to talk to me, refused to even consider—"

"People are asleep!" Jen hissed at him. "You might lower your voice."

Pierre smiled, reached for her and drew her close. "And you might lower yours . . ."

Jen squirmed away, infuriated by her response to his virility. Damn sex! Damn him!

"It's not funny!" she snapped, unmindful of the rise in her voice.

"I know it isn't!" Pierre shouted. "Damn it, Jenifer, I wouldn't have expected this sort of hysterical behavior from . . ."

"Oh, you thought I was still the naive, mute little fumbling creature you rescued in Paris . . . !"

"Will you stop talking . . . !"

"No!" Jen's eyes blazed. "I don't know what happened between you and Catherine this weekend and I don't want to know. Damn you for coming here." She lowered her voice to a lethal whisper. "Damn you for making all this so public!"

"Listen!" He grabbed for her arm but she darted inside the house and ran upstairs. She heard him behind her, taking the stairs three at a time. By the time she reached her door he was beside her. He shoved her inside, slamming the door closed behind him. He stood with his back to the door, glaring at her.

175

"I would never accuse you of being naive, or fumbling as you say," Pierre told her. "That is how you have seen yourself. I have never seen you that way."

Jen turned away with tears stinging in her eyes. Everything was out of control. She felt herself trembling.

"This reaction from you has shocked me, Jenifer." Pierre spoke in a low voice now. "Perhaps it has hurt my confidence in you as my . . . apparent behavior has hurt yours in me. I thought you knew me. Thought you knew me well enough to know I would never intentionally hurt you. How can you doubt me this much . . . how can you get so caught up in appearances?"

"How can you expect me not to?" Jen turned to him tearfully. "It's asking too much of me not to have doubts when you show up with your beautiful ex-wife, a woman who is . . . really . . . really . . . one of the most beautiful . . ."

"But I love you . . . I've told you so."

"You love me"—Jen bit back her tears—"but there is no future. I've heard your words of love. I've heard them and I believed them. I did believe you loved me. But what about our future? You scarcely talk about our future. Any talk was only empty words. So . . . is it any wonder that when Catherine appeared I might consider your words about her only that? Words!"

"They were more than words," Pierre whispered.

"How could I have known that?" Jen asked desperately.

"Dammit, I love you!" Pierre hurled the declaration out with a frustrated wave of his hand.

"I'm flying back to Iowa in three . . . four days

. . . and you've said not one word about what will happen then . . ."

"I've done little else but think about our future. Would you please read this?" Pierre dug into the pocket of his trench coat and shoved an early edition of *Le Figaro* into her hands. "Third column, halfway down," he said bitterly.

Jen took in the headline with a faint gasp: "Pierre Rennes, one of France's most distinguished and inventive young chefs, relinquishes ownership of La Petite Auberge."

"What . . . ?" Jen sank onto the bed and stared inquiringly into his embittered eyes.

"I went to Paris last weekend and the time before . . . to talk to Catherine. Rather, to *try* to talk to Catherine . . . which is something of an impossibility." He sighed in exasperation. "You see, at the dissolution of our marriage there was a settlement. Our settlement stated that, as we had both invested our time and talents in La Petite Auberge, we owned equal shares. However, upon the remarriage of either party the remaining party would have the option to buy the other out. As I should like to remarry, Catherine now is in the position of buying me out . . . which is what she intends to do. So you see, Jenifer, I not only love you . . . in words. I want to marry you with my whole heart . . . with my entire life."

177

CHAPTER ELEVEN

"If you remarry . . . if you marry me . . . ?" Jen sprang to her feet and stared at Pierre with astonishment.

Pierre nodded. "That's right. You understand now."

"If you marry me . . . you'll lose La Petite Auberge?"

"Catherine has decided to exercise her option." Pierre tried in vain to smile.

"But it's not fair!" Jen exclaimed. "It's your restaurant. Everyone knows that. You made it what it is. It's your profession, not Catherine's. She's not a chef, she's . . ."

Ma chère . . ." Pierre drew her gently against his chest and held her there, softly caressing her forehead, as if she were the one in need of soothing. "I so much did not want it to happen like this." He brushed his lips against the top of her head. "A proposal should be joyous. I wanted it to be that. I want to marry you, Jen. More than anything in the world I want us to have a life together."

"You can't give up La Petite Auberge," Jen insisted as she looked up at him.

"I've no choice." Pierre managed a faint smile. "I am, after all, a gentleman of principle. I place love above all else. I can always make another restaurant."

"It's not fair!" Jen cried, pacing across the room. "You can fight it . . . legally."

"No." Pierre shook his head. "It was all settled when the divorce was finalized."

"But it's not fair!" Jen exclaimed again.

"But she wants it," Pierre said grimly, "and that is enough for Catherine."

"I'm so sorry . . ." Jen walked over to him slowly and took his hands in hers. "Pierre, please forgive me for doubting you." So it really was true. All of the pictures Pierre kept of his beautiful ex-wife were there to remind him of how vindictive she could be.

"I was so sure I could convince her." Pierre gave a defeated shrug.

"How could anyone be so . . ." Jen broke off with a distasteful expression.

"Jenifer, it was you who taught me how to let go of my bitterness. Now is not the time to renew it. In all fairness, Catherine contributed enormously to the Auberge, especially in the early years of our marriage when we were both struggling to make a name. She poured much of her own money into the place, and when she gained an international reputation in films, she and the film crowd she ran around with lent an air of glamour to the place. Because I was married to her I was more than just another superior chef. No, I do not begrudge Catherine her share . . . only her vindictiveness in waiting me out."

"What do you mean . . . waiting you out?"

"Catherine has been living with someone for several years . . . since after the divorce. I'm quite sure she would have married him by now were it not for the terms of the divorce settlement. But please . . ." Pierre wrapped his arms around Jen and tilted her chin upward. "The most important question has been left dangling . . ."

"I will marry you!" Jen's face broke into a smile.

"We can make a new Auberge." Pierre began kissing her fiercely. "We will!"

"Of course we will!" Jen felt the tears streaming down her face as he tumbled her onto the bed. "I love you so, Pierre! You know that, don't you?"

Her body surged with the urgent need to communicate, as words never could, the full spectrum of her passion and love. In a frenzy of passionate kissing, they quickly undressed. Jen's hands glided artfully along his warm muscular body. Never had his flesh felt so dear, never had she felt such abandon in opening herself to him.

Pierre's mouth moved across her breasts, leaving her tingling and twisting in a blind ecstasy. With the adroitness of one possessed, Jen guided him against her supple curves, softly crying out as he filled her. My wildest dreams . . . she arched into him and welcomed his powerful thrusts.

She opened her eyes, watching his face as he moved over her. His eyes were closed tight, his face flushed with sensual pleasure. Looking at him aroused her to even greater heights, inflaming her so that her body trembled with delight.

"Ma chère . . ." Pierre murmured huskily.

"Yes!" she cried as she felt her body swell at his touch. His body tensed in readiness, and just as another cataclysmic tremor shook her, he fell forward, burying his dark head against her shoulder.

Jen caressed his broad shoulders as he lay against her, breathing heavily. Finally he rolled to one side and gave her a dazed but happy look. "We will be married soon. I must be properly introduced to the boys. Tomorrow we will make plans . . ."

"Yes," Jen cuddled against him and kissed him softly as his eyelids fluttered shut. For a moment she listened to the rapid beating of his heart as it slowed to its normal rhythm. Then she pulled the covers over them and fell asleep.

She woke abruptly the next morning. Pierre was still sleeping soundly beside her. The warm erotic feelings which had shielded Jen the night before had evaporated. In the cold light of day the thought of Pierre's losing La Petite Auberge felt like a death to her.

She glanced at her watch. It was already eight o'clock. Usually Pierre was at the restaurant by this time. She eased herself out of bed and looked down at him with a resolute expression. Then she dressed in a pair of jeans and her navy-blue sweatshirt. Pierre needed his sleep. Michel could assume charge at Auberge. Let him wake in his own good time. Meanwhile, she knew what she had to do.

Since Eric had so gleefully reported that Catherine's car was parked at Pierre's house, she assumed the film star was staying there. A faint smile crossed her face as she realized that that titillating piece of gossip no longer held any threat to her. She tiptoed down the back stairs, let herself out of Madame Pauline's and after a moment's hesitation walked into the center of town and

181

found a taxi cab. She did not want to risk missing Catherine and it would take at least an hour on her bike.

The day was gray and bleak. She watched the rock-mulched vineyards flash by and tried not to think of what she intended to say to Catherine Rennes. The driver left her off at the end of the lane that led to Pierre's house. Her heart quickened at the sight of Catherine's limousine. Leaving the cab, Jen walked up the lane, listening to the birds in the misty green fields.

She hesitated as she approached the back door. Maybe she would sit on the stoop and wait for some sign of life rather than risk waking her. Just at that moment, however, Catherine Rennes's pale, delicate face appeared at the door.

Momentarily, Jen froze. "I must speak with you," Jen burst out in French, praying that her grasp of the language would be sufficient enough to express herself.

"Oui." Catherine gave a quick, quizzical smile as she opened the door. "I have made coffee," she replied in hesitant English.

"Thank you." Jen smiled and sat down at Pierre's old wooden table.

"I did not expect you." Catherine handed Jen the coffee with a surprisingly candid expression in her large sea-gray eyes.

"And I don't know what I'm going to say." Jen looked directly at the other woman, feeling for the briefest moment a totally unexpected and most extraordinary bond between them. It occurred to her that long ago the beautiful woman seated across from her had loved Pierre Rennes. That was the bond and it was a very real one.

"There must be some way!" Jen jumped in. "You

182

know Pierre is aware of how much you contributed to La Petite Auberge. Last night, when he
finally told me what was going on between you
two, I was the one who wanted to cry "bitch,
money-grubber" . . . not Pierre."

"Of course you would want to say that." Catherine lowered her eyes wearily and took a sip of
coffee. "I am a bit of both, I suppose."

Jen contemplated the surprising acknowledg-
ment for a moment. "But why? If it is the money,
I'm sure Pierre would work out some new financial arrangement. Or perhaps a new settlement
can be reached where you could remain his partner. That way you would continue to share in the
profits."

Catherine looked up with a faint, admiring
smile. "Are you a businesswoman, then? Pierre
did not say."

"No, no. I can't claim to being anything really
. . . except a mother of three sons. I came over
here with the hope of getting my life together in
order to support them."

Catherine stared into her coffee and for a moment Jen thought she was going to cry. "You have
made things very difficult for me by coming here,"
Catherine said after a long pause.

"I had to come."

Catherine nodded. After another thoughtful
pause she looked up with an incredulous smile.
"You seem like a very interesting woman," she
said frankly.

Jen felt her cheeks flush but, perhaps for the first
time in her life, there was no embarrassment connected with the blush.

"But that doesn't mean I'm giving in." Catherine assumed a cool attitude.

183

"Maybe you'll think about it. . . . Maybe the idea of remaining partners could work?"

"You wouldn't feel odd about that?" Catherine queried.

Jen shook her head. "It might be the best solution for both you and Pierre."

"And you? Would it be best for you to have a ghost from Pierre's past flitting around?" There was a note of sarcasm in Catherine's voice.

"As long as you behave yourself!" Jen grinned unexpectedly. Catherine looked up with a surprised expression and laughed.

"Well . . ." The Frenchwoman bobbed her head dramatically as her large eyes swept around Pierre's kitchen. "Pierre told you I have had a . . . a liaison with another man for some time?"

Jen nodded.

"And yet you haven't mentioned it?" Catherine remarked.

"It didn't seem relevant." Jen shrugged. She saw what Catherine was getting at: Jen had not walked in and started blaming her, had never once put the Frenchwoman on the defensive.

Catherine bobbed her head again. "I will think about what you've said."

Jenifer did not tell Pierre about her visit with Catherine. She met him after the morning class for a brief walk in the woods. They rustled through russet-colored autumnal leaves, holding hands, speaking very little. A sense of bittersweet melancholy pervaded their happiness. Jen's love for the Frenchman swelled each time she thought of how much he was willing to give up. Although he was trying valiantly to make the best of the situation, there was no way he could hide his feelings from Jen. She squeezed his hand reassuringly. Silently

184

she cautioned herself not to hold out too much hope where Catherine was concerned. True, the meeting had taken an unexpectedly smooth course, but from all Pierre had told her she knew Catherine was a woman of many faces. Jen would have to be prepared for the worst and somehow she would have to support Pierre in his decision.

"I've been in touch with a wonderful tutor for the boys," he told her as they walked along a little meandering brook. "Of course I want to spend time in Duffy. Certainly I'll fly back with you. But then, of course, I shall have to begin looking around for a new spot. I've been thinking of the north . . . say Normandy, where I grew up. You'll love it there. Or perhaps the best plan is for us to drive around the country together. It will be your choice, too."

She bit back her desire to give him some hope that Catherine might reconsider her ultimatum and listened to him detail his plans for opening a new Auberge in another part of France.

"This is a damned way to begin making our happy plans!" Finally the frustration was too much for him and he burst out angrily, storming off.

Jen ran after him. "Don't worry. I know you're happy about us. I'm not confusing things. How could you be jumping for joy when everything you've worked for is going to be taken away from you?"

"Well, she's paying a pretty sum for it," Pierre said bitterly.

"I intend to make it all worth your while." Jen looked into his gloomy face with a soft smile. "I won't let you regret your choice."

Pierre fell against her and held her. When he looked at her again his cragged face was composed and there was even a twinkle in his eye. "I have more bad news." He smiled.

"Wonderful!" Jen clapped her hands. "I can hardly wait for more!"

"That is"—he took her hand, swinging it back and forth as they walked—"you stand a very good chance of winning first prize. Did you know that?"

Jen blushed. "Well . . . yes."

"You did!" Pierre whirled her off the ground. "I see your ego has bloomed under French skies. And you keep it so well hidden!"

"Well, I'd thought of it. I mean . . . . I'm *one* of the best but . . ."

"The bad news is, I should prefer that you didn't win. At this rather vulnerable juncture of my life I should hate to encounter any more criticism. It would be terrible to be suspected of favoritism. Is it asking terribly much of you, Jen, to withdraw from this competition? I mean . . . there will be other prizes to win. I want you to go on, you know, and make your own name but . . ."

"Of course!" Jen interrupted jubilantly. "Pierre, I've won so much more than I ever thought I would. And I promise, there will be other competitions and I will win them!"

"I see you've learned to rather enjoy the competition . . . the idea of winning appeals to you, does it?"

"It certainly does!" Jen hugged him.

"I want to make love to you right now!" Pierre was immediately aroused. His hands swept down the sides of her body and his mouth opened onto hers in a deep penetrating kiss.

His thick tongue teased deep into her mouth, setting off an explosion of fiery memories. As he lowered her to the ground, behind a stand of evergreens, he artfully unzipped her jeans and began stroking the smooth expanse of her stomach.

"I want to make love to you everywhere! In the mountains!" He kissed her intensely. "By the sea. In your Iowa cornfields!" His hands roamed across her quivering body until she could scarcely bear the pleasure.

"Pierre!" Half laughing, she tried to restrain him.

"No one will come! I promise! You've dreamed of this moment. . . . Remember?" He pressed against her. "That first afternoon, our first picnic?"

"I remember . . ." Jen moaned as he deftly freed her of her jeans and panties.

"Everywhere I will make love to you . . ." Seconds later she felt his warm body on top of her, felt the longing in him. "In the kitchen!"

She laughed exuberantly and met his eyes as he moved over her, affirming with each passionate thrust all that their new life together would mean. Suddenly it was as if they had both been released from the dark cloud hovering over them. Their bodies were connected now more passionately and completely than ever before. And they were laughing!

There was no word from Catherine that afternoon, nor the following morning, the day of the competition and the gala banquet. As she dressed for the evening's festivities Jen gazed wonderingly at her reflection in the mirror. Her hair was swept back away from her face in a sleek chignon to accentuate the tiny drop diamond earrings that Pierre had laughingly "awarded" her. Also, at Pierre's insistence she had gone back to the boutique and purchased a slinky gray gown that had

187

captured her fancy some days before. What, she wondered with an impish smile, would Meryl Beamen make of her now? She stared harder at herself. The folks back home might say she'd changed, but the funny thing was, she felt more herself than she had ever felt in her life.

There was a knock at her door. Thinking it was probably Nellie, Jen called, "Come in." Much to her surprise, Catherine Rennes appeared before her. She entered the room, closing the door behind her.

"I'm selling my share to Pierre," she announced firmly, staring at Jen with determination. "I want you to tell him," she said. Jen gestured for her to sit down. Catherine shook her head. "I'm on my way back to Paris. Your visit yesterday helped me to finally see things as they are. I won't go into the details. Let's just say Pierre and I were both embittered by our failed marriage. I as much as he. I know you know his side . . . that's as it should be. Anyway, we both wanted to hurt the other. My sole reason for insisting on the option to buy Pierre out should he remarry first was based on nothing but revenge. Unfortunately, as I'm sure you know, that's not an uncommon motive in divorcing couples. I really didn't much like myself for it and . . . I guess when you told me that Pierre valued my input in the restaurant . . . something he, in his own bitterness, could not bring himself to tell me . . . well, it made me remember some of the good times between us. You must know what I mean." Catherine paused wistfully. "You were married before. There are good times . . . even in a rotten marriage."

"I do know." Jen nodded.

"So I said . . . to hell with this game. It's time

to put aside bitterness. Just tell Pierre to contact my lawyer. He'll pay a stiff price for my share"— she smiled—"but not unreasonable."

"Shouldn't you tell him . . . ?"

"I think you should." Catherine stood with her hand on the doorknob, then extended her hand. "I honestly wish you the best."

As she was leaving she turned back to Jen with an ironic smile. "I must say, I don't envy you sharing a kitchen with Pierre." Then she was gone.

Jen stood for a moment staring at the door in astonishment. She looked around wildly, her excitement practically uncontainable. She had to find Pierre! She grabbed a canvas tote, threw her heels inside and put on a pair of sneakers. She hiked the gray dress up nicely and tied a scarf around her waist to hold it in place, tossed on her coat, went downstairs and hopped on her bike.

What a picture she must have presented: diamond earrings and sneakers, a grown woman with the wind tearing through her hair, pedaling demonically through the autumn dusk! Six weeks ago she would have been a nervous wreck at the idea of wearing a slinky gray dress and meeting the culinary giants who would be gathered at this evening's function. Now, she thought with a grin, she was "sophisticated" enough to arrive on a bike wearing sneakers!

However, she was not *so* sophisticated that she wasn't relieved that no one saw her straining up the final incline to the Auberge. She parked her bike in its usual place, exchanged sneakers for heels, ordered her hair, let down the hiked-up dress and hurried to the narrow door to Pierre's kitchen. She knew the place would be a flurry of

189

ectic dinner activity, that no one *ever* interrupted the master chef during these crucial hours.

"Pierre!" She thrust her head inside, smiling more broadly at the dazzling conglomeration of aromas. "Pierre!" She ignored the incredulous stares of Michel and the other assistants who were bustling around.

Pierre, attired in full white chef's attire, was standing over the stove. He shook his head and waved her off. Then sensing she was still there, he signaled Michel to take over and strode over to Jen with a perplexed expression.

Jen could not help laughing as she pulled him outside and closed the door. He was infuriated by the interruption.

"Pierre . . ." she gasped, "Catherine has changed her mind! She just came to tell me. She will sell to you! At a fair price!"

The anger drained from Pierre's face. He stood staring at Jen with a blank expression. For an instant she thought he was going to cry.

". . . you went to talk to her . . . ?" Jen nodded, watching his face as he pieced together what must have happened. "I thought she would take her revenge to the grave." He shook his head with a dazed expression. "What did you say to her?"

Jen looked at him evenly. "I told Catherine some of the decent things you'd said about her, how her name had helped build the business, how, deep in your heart, you recognized that the Auberge had been her dream as well as yours. I just told her the truth and I suggested a compromise—that she continue as your partner and share in the profits. I didn't ask her to give up anything. That was her idea." Jen felt a deep thrill as the light returned to Pierre's eyes.

"My God . . . !" Pierre gathered her against his white apron and held her. "What can I say?" He looked at her with tears in his eyes.

Nothing. He didn't need to say a word. It was all written in his strong, loving face as he bent down and kissed her.

"As far as I'm concerned"—he held her away from him with an awed expression—"you are the only woman with whom I will *ever* share my kitchen."